Also by Jas͏ ͏ ͏ ͏ ͏

Smell & Bogey and the Missing Slippers

Smell & Bogey
and the Magic Carpet

Jason Moss

Illustrated by Steven Hier

Visit Smell & Bogey at:
www.smellandbogey.com

Published in 2011 by New Generation Publishing

For Mum & Dad

To Abigail,

Enjoy all the snottyness!

Preface

Have you ever wondered what lives in the carpet under your feet? Take a look… a good close look… there's another world down there, a miniature world full of weird and wonderful things you wouldn't believe, a place full of adventure where the strangest things happen, and they often happen to Smell and Bogey.

Smell and Bogey lived deep in the Magic Carpet in a little green Monopoly house surrounded by the tall woolly threads of the magical rug, which towered above them like a forest.

Bogey liked a quiet life; he also liked eating, sleeping and tidying up.

Smell, on the other hand, craved adventure; he was always looking for excitement and often getting into trouble.

One fairly quiet day with nothing much going on, apart from something getting right up Bogey's nose, 'KNOCK-KNOCK-KNOCK!' Someone came to visit Smell and Bogey who would kick-start an adventure so wild and fantastic even Smell had never dreamt of such excitement.

Chapter One

Snot Mouth

'Aaahhh-tis-sue!!' sneezed Bogey for the forty-eighth time.

'Oh no, no more, please, no more. Aaahhh-tissue!!' he sneezed again as splutter shot from his mouth covering the kitchen table, narrowly avoiding the biscuits that sat waiting to be eaten.

Then there was silence, once the crockery and the pots and the pans on the kitchen dresser had finally stopped wobbling from all the commotion.

Smell looked at Bogey with hope in his eyes. 'He must've sneezed himself dry by now?' he thought, 'No-one can sneeze forty-nine times and not need a break.'

He'd tried waving every type of biscuit in front of Bogey's face in the hope he would stop sneezing, but even the most delicious treacle and chocolate chip cookies had no effect.

Bogey was a rosy-cheeked, pop-bellied, cuddly sort of character. If you had to cuddle a bogey, Bogey would be the one to cuddle. He had a faded greenish complexion, a bit shrivelled around the edges, with one of those faces you warm to straight away.

By now he was bent over in exhaustion, panting and spluttering. His whole face had turned a bright red to match his cheeks and his big bulging belly was covered in splutter and splatter and snot and dribble.

Smell decided Bogey must be finished sneezing and opened his mouth to speak… but, oh yes, you've guessed it, as soon as Smell opened his mouth, an ear-piercingly enormous... no, gigantic... no, bigger than that… the loudest sneeze you have ever heard in your life exploded with all the thrust and force of a jet engine, catapulting Bogey half way across the kitchen floor and splattering poor old Smell with all the snot and dribble you can imagine.

A moment of peace and calm descended in the kitchen as the dust settled. On one side of the room lay Bogey, exhausted but relieved he'd stopped sneezing; on the other lay Smell, a squiggly gooey mess, covered from head to toe in Bogey's slime.

Smell was normally quite a slender, transparent chap. He did change shape every now and then depending on which way the wind was blowing; their next-door neighbour Fluff had recently described him as very good-looking, something which Smell was very proud of. It didn't make him popular with the ladies, mind, because there was always a rather strong waft coming from his general direction. If you must know, the smell that Smell smells of is smelly feet – just a gentle pong.

His mouth was wide open in shock, dribbling and oozing, he looked more like a snot ball than a smell.

He stared at Bogey in anger.

'Why does he never use a handkerchief?' he thought as he picked himself up off the kitchen floor.

Bogey by now was straightening all the wall pictures that had been blown wonky in the hullabaloo.

'You and your smelly feet!' cried Bogey.

'Me!' exclaimed Smell in surprise. 'You're blaming me? I'm not the one with a nose like a gale force wind!'

Bogey rested his arms on his big bulging belly as he looked around the room. His enormous tummy made a very handy arm rest at times. There was a sense of satisfaction and achievement on his face, then a big cheeky grin started to appear.

'Well at least I've stopped sneezing, Smelly! Fifty times in one go – that's got to be a carpet record surely?' he announced with pride as he mopped up the dribble from his belly.

Smell rolled his eyes. 'It's nothing to be proud of… and anyway, I heard of a girl that sneezed every day of her life for ten years until she stopped.'

'Really? How *did* she stop?'

'She sneezed herself to death! On her tenth birthday it was… very sad.'

Bogey looked at Smell with a disgruntled frown.

'Thank you, Snotty!'

Smell giggled to himself as he noticed dribble dangling on the end of his big toe.

'Look at the mess everywhere!' he cried as he started to rummage around his mouth with his tongue, fishing for something.

Bogey realised there was much to do and got to doing it. There were snot piles and dribble everywhere! Dangling from the light shades, dribbling down the cupboards and oozing all over the kitchen sink.

'I do hope I didn't snot on the biscuits! I was looking forward to them.'

He started looking around the room for snot piles. You won't believe how far snot can travel when it's shooting out of your nose at one hundred miles per hour. It gets everywhere!

'Don't think you're getting out of tidying up!' shouted Bogey.

Smell was still in the corner of the room, still rummaging around his mouth. By now he'd got his hands stuck down his throat frantically looking for something.

'What *are* you doing?' cried Bogey as Smell finally found what he'd been looking for. He pulled something out of his mouth and took one good long look at it sitting on the tips of his fingers. And then...

'AAAARGH!!' He exploded into a frenzy, jumping around the kitchen like a cricket on a pogo stick.

'Aargh...urgh...splurr...splutter!' He spat and shook his head wildly, wiping his hands on his trousers in disgust.

'Mind the teapot!' yelled Bogey, catching it just in time.

'Mind the biscuits!' he cried, trying to shield them from any more dribble. 'I'm not eating them if you've snotted all over them!' Smell was coughing and spluttering all over the place, now *his* face was turning a pinky-red.

'What *is* the matter with you?' Bogey demanded.

Scraping his tongue frantically, Smell looked at Bogey and screamed, 'I've got a mouth full of your snot!! That's what's up with me!' He let out an enormous noisy shudder, shivering in revulsion.

'Waaaobble! You're gross Bogey, you really are,' he whimpered, feeling sorry for himself.

'It's your smelly feet that start me off, Snot-mouth,' said Bogey as he got on with the tidying up, feeling just that little bit guilty.

Once Bogey had got the kitchen looking a little cleaner, and Smell had spent at least twenty minutes or so scrubbing and wiping every part of his mouth and face, they both settled down at the kitchen table, exhausted from the morning's commotion.

Bogey yawned as he stared vacantly at the biscuits set on the kitchen table.

'What shall we have for tea?' he thought, as his bulging belly let out an enormous hungry growl.

Smell was scraping away at his two front teeth with his fingernail, still obsessively cleaning. His belly also started to rumble. He suddenly stopped and stared at Bogey with eyes wide open.

'What?' cried Bogey, looking spooked.

'Can you hear that?'

'What?'

'That noise!'

'What noise?'

'That noise, listen!!'

'That's your hungry belly!'

'No! No... that noise, listen!'

They both froze and listened as a faint, rhythmic noise slowly increased in volume.

'It's coming from the kitchen floor – listen!' said Smell, positively elated that something exciting was happening.

Thud – Thump – Thud – Thump – THUD – THUMP – THUD – THUMP!! It *was* getting louder. The kitchen floor had started to shudder, the table was wobbling and the biscuits were definitely shaking.

Smell suddenly took in an almighty gasp of air. He'd been concentrating so hard on the noise that he'd forgotten to breathe!

'What do you think it is, Boges?' He put his ear to the kitchen floor to get a better listen.

'It sounds like marching feet or an engine or something,' replied Bogey, not that interested. If it didn't involve food it wasn't worth getting that excited over.

Then, suddenly, it stopped. The kitchen was silent again. Smell's mouth was wide open in wonder.

'Err, close that! Tar very much!' shouted Bogey, pointing at Smell's gaping mouth.

'Growwlll!' went his stomach again, as he focused back on the biscuits.

After five minutes or so with his head glued to the kitchen floor, Smell gave up listening, sat back down at the kitchen table and also stared back at the biscuits.

'I wonder what snotty biscuits taste like?' he thought, as he started to count them one by one.

'Nine, ten, eleven, twelve!' he counted in his head.

Bogey, not surprisingly, was thinking the same thing, although he'd counted them at least twelve times already.

They both stared at the snotty biscuits and then at each other.

Who would give in first?

Smell started to drool and dribble as the thought of snotty biscuits became more and more appealing.

'Oi!' shouted Bogey, pointing at Smell's oozing chops. 'We've had enough of that for one day, tar.' Smell turned to wipe his face, then cleaned his slobbery hands on his trousers.

'Nine, ten, eleven... Oi! Where's number twelve?' he screamed, realising one was now missing. 'You've eaten number twelve!'

'I have not!'

'Yes you have, there were twelve there a minute ago and now there's only eleven!'

'Ooh, look at the professor go!' Bogey exclaimed sarcastically.

'I counted twelve and now there's only eleven!' Smell was getting unusually passionate over food; normally it was the other way around.

'Well, I haven't had one!'

Then suddenly from the other side of the kitchen came an odd sort of noise.

'Boing!'

Smell and Bogey both looked towards the sound.

'Ka-boing!' went the noise again.

'What is it?' asked Bogey, peering over the kitchen table, slightly worried in case it was a mouse, or something worse like a spider or a big creepy bug. He wasn't fond of bugs. The last time a bug found its way into the house he spent the whole day standing on the kitchen table, with his knees wobbling. He had good reason, it was a pretty creepy bug with thirteen eyes, three noses and it jumped so fast you never knew where it would land next. And every time it did jump it would make a loud farting noise. It was only after Bogey accidentally sat on it that the thing met its end. Or, rather, Bogey's end.

Life in the Magic Carpet could be fun most of the time, but every now and then some weird thing would land on the carpet and cause havoc and destruction. The carpet possessed magical powers that nobody understood. Take Smell and Bogey for example. When was the last time you saw a bogey walking? When was the last time you heard a smell talking?

It doesn't normally happen, but when you live in the Magic Carpet, the impossible becomes possible.

'Ka-boing!' went the sound yet again.

'Look at that!' screamed Smell, pointing to the kitchen floor.

'What?' whimpered Bogey, as he covered his ears in fear.

'Look at that!' Smell screamed again with excitement, pointing to the corner of the kitchen in disbelief.

The twelfth biscuit had sprouted arms and legs and was running for his life, as fast as his little legs would carry him. He was heading for the crack in the kitchen wall. He was quick too. If biscuits ran in the Olympics, this little Hobnob would take gold.

Quicker than you could say 'fast-food', Smell and Bogey leapt from their seats and hurled themselves toward the little Hobnob, determined to win back their tasty treat.

CRASH – BANG – WOLLOP!! went Smell, Bogey and the kitchen chairs, ending up in a tangled heap on the floor.

'I've got him, I've got him!' screamed Smell in excitement. His hands were cupped over something on the kitchen floor. Sticking out from his fingers were two little biscuity-legs wriggling frantically trying to get free.

'Oh, well done, Smelly boy!' Bogey announced triumphantly, as he tried to remove his head from one of the kitchen chairs.

The little biscuit was wriggling for his life, like a helpless fly trapped by a hungry predator.

URR-GURGLE! went Bogey's belly as he managed to free his head from the awkward chair leg. Immediately, Smell's tummy made a similar sound.

WORR-GUR-RUMBLE! Their bellies were in perfect rhythm.

'I think we better tuck into these biscuits before they all start running for freedom.'

'Good idea, I'm starving!' said Smell.

Bogey brewed a pot of English breakfast tea and Smell laid out all the biscuits neatly on a fresh, clean plate. He'd tied the one with the legs to a separate plate with string; he was still frantically wriggling away.

Bogey poured a cup of tea for himself and then one for Smell. He was eying up the largest biscuit on the plate.

'I'll have that one!' he signalled with his big beady eyes while pouring the tea.

Then suddenly the most extraordinary thing happened. All the biscuits on the plate started to shake. Then they started to shudder.

And then with an almighty rumble, then a pop, every biscuit on the plate suddenly sprouted arms. It was the strangest sight.

POP! went one biscuit. *PING!* went another. There were arms everywhere. Imagine it, eleven hysterical biscuits suddenly discovering the use of their arms. Every biscuit on the plate started waving frantically in excitement – what a commotion!

One biscuit accidentally hit another one on the head, causing it to fall off the plate. Another biscuit had managed to use his hands as feet, and was running around the kitchen table like a wild monkey. Smell and Bogey just stared in amazement watching the mayhem unfold before their very eyes. Smell started to giggle at one wriggling around the kitchen table dragging his long, dangly arms behind him. Another two had started fighting as if they were in a boxing ring. Another one looked like he was running as fast as he could, but having no legs he was going nowhere very slowly. There were arms flying all over the place.

If that wasn't enough, suddenly all eleven excited biscuits sprouted legs!

POP, PING, PRANG, PONG!

'Weeeeeeeee!!' went all the biscuits as they discovered what you could do with legs.

'RUN!' cried one eager Hobnob, and all the biscuits jumped to their new-found feet and scarpered.

WHOOOSH! There were biscuits all over the place, jumping off the kitchen table, darting across the kitchen floor, sliding down the chair legs, all scurrying to find a hiding place.

Bogey immediately let out an almighty, girly scream and jumped onto the kitchen table in fright.

'Ooohhh no!' he cried, raising his hands in the air, knees wobbling in horror.

The tied-up biscuit, Number Twelve, suddenly managed to wriggle free. By now there was hardly a single biscuit in sight and Number Twelve was eager to join his crumbly chums. This time, he ran even faster than before.

Determined not to lose the only biscuit left, Smell made one almighty leap from his chair.

WHOOOSH! He glided through the air, like a smelly gust of wind in slow motion.

CRASH! BANG! WALLOP! He landed on the kitchen dresser, knocking off all the crockery.

CLANG! BANG! SMASH! CRASH! went the cups and the plates as they fell to the floor…

As the dust settled in the kitchen for a second time that morning, Smell lay upside down with his head stuck in the kitchen dresser drawer, legs dangling in the air, dazed from the whole experience and covered in bits of broken bowls and plates.

Bogey was still standing on the kitchen table, knees wobbling, with his hands over his ears in fright. He looked over at Smell, and took one look at his feet waving in the air. And then…

'AAAHHH – TISSS – UUUEEE!!!'

Chapter Two

KNOCK-KNOCK-KNOCK!

Deep in the Magic Carpet, where the threads were worn thin, there was a place known as 'Dribble's Leap'. Nobody ever went there much, mainly because it was dangerous. The middle of the carpet was the one place where you'd most likely get trodden on, eaten alive or disappear. Several friends had gone missing around Dribble's Leap. It was named Dribble's Leap after the famous disappearance of Dribble, a character very popular in these parts long before Smell and Bogey's time. And although it happened a long time ago, everybody knew the story.

Dribble had set out to look for his friend Fluff, who'd gone missing after one of her trips. Fluff liked to travel and was often gallivanting… She didn't have much choice, mind – she was so light and fluffy that whenever there was a gust of wind, she would just blow off.

WHOOOSH!

Fluff had been gone for days at a time before, but on this occasion she'd been gone a whole week and Dribble had started to worry.

So he decided to search the carpet. He walked through the Magic Carpet for days and days, asking everybody he met if they'd seen her... but nobody had. The last time Dribble was ever seen was by the worn out thread in the middle of the Magic Carpet. No-one knows what really happened to Dribble: some say he was trodden on by the humans, others say he just gave up hope and jumped through the bare threads of the carpet and into the pit below. You were doomed if you fell into the pit. All sorts of creepy creatures lived down there in the dark, and besides, there was no way back up once you'd fallen in.

From that day to this, the place where the carpet was worn thin and bare was known as 'Dribble's Leap'. The carpet had become so thin that there were big holes which anyone could fall through. If you were foolish enough to try to cross, the only way over was to take a long run-up and leap.

Fluff did eventually return. She'd been caught by a rather gusty breeze and floated off outside through the window. After a week of floating around the back garden she managed to get back to the Magic Carpet. She'd landed on the back of old Ginger Bags, the cat. Ginger Bags always took a nap on the Magic Carpet, by the fireplace at approximately twelve-ish each day, so Fluff was lucky this time.

Fluff was very upset after hearing about Dribble. It was only when Smell and Bogey moved next door to her that she started to enjoy life again.

Afternoon was always a quiet time in the Magic Carpet. The humans were at school, or out somewhere buying more stuff. The cat by the fireplace was well and truly fast asleep after his morning hike downstairs to eat breakfast, which always made old Ginger Bags very tired. And the carpet was at its warmest after the midday sun had heated every fibre and particle in its path. Most of the carpet's residents usually fell fast asleep at this time. The sun's rays would send everyone into a drowsy, sleepy daze; even Smell couldn't fight it. He'd tried once… he'd decided to see how long he could stay awake once the sun came out. He started counting… but only remembers getting up to number three…

The sound of snoring echoed throughout the entire carpet that afternoon. Smell and Bogey sounded like they were having a *Who can snore the loudest* competition after such an exhausting morning with the runaway biscuits and all. Bogey was definitely winning.

All was still. Noisy, but still… except for two dark figures climbing up through the worn out threads at Dribble's Leap.

Who - or what - were they?

'SSSHHH,' whispered the hooded figure, as he helped his mate up through a gap in the worn-out carpet.

HICCUP! went his friend, who was also wearing a hooded cloak, but his outfit looked a little on the large side. He kept pulling up his sleeves and rearranging himself. You could only just make out their faces: they were very thin and scrawny with pointed noses. But the one thing that did stand out was their horrible red glowing-eyes, permanently fixed in an evil stare.

'What's that?' the baggy one cried out, listening to the noises coming from deep within the thick forest of carpet that surrounded them.

'SSHHH, it's just everyone snoring,' the smaller one said. He seemed the wiser of the two. He started to survey the bare patch of carpet that lay before them, checking no-one had seen them arrive. He hopped around Dribble's Leap with a strange sideways limp.

'What ya doing?' whispered the taller one.

'I'm checking the coast is clear, now SSHH!'

'Are we by the sea?'

'Will you shut up, Finch!'

'Eh?' said Finch, putting his strange, claw-like hand to his pointed ears.

'Shut... UP!' the other one shouted, as a few disturbed moans were heard coming from the carpet.

The smaller one peered into the thick forest of threads that circled them, towering above them like pine trees.

'Is the tide out, Herron?' asked Finch.

'What?' said Herron, distracted from his surveillance.

'Is the tide out, then?'

Herron walked up to Finch, who towered over him like a scrawny, giant twig with arms. He looked up and stared at him wildly with his big, blood-red eyeballs bulging. Finch flinched and new he'd better shut up pronto - he only ever got that look when he'd said *something* wrong.

'No sea, then,' he said, hoping it would calm Herron down. *HICCUP!*

'Will you stop hiccupping and be quiet, please! Now listen... Plan B is to swarm into the north and...'

He continued to tell Finch Plan B in such a whisper only dogs could hear him.

Herron finished whispering.

'Now... have you got that?'

'Yes,' said Finch. 'We warm up on the Tuesday and make casserole, then feed trout to the pensioners, tickling the cat with everything we've got.' *HICCUP!*

'Never mind, Finch,' said Herron. 'I wasn't expecting you to understand. All I need you to do is follow instructions and listen carefully, OK?'

'Eh?'

Herron and Finch continued their plotting and planning that afternoon. Who were they, and what were they up to?

'What's that?' Finch cried out, looking up at the tops of the carpet swaying in the breeze. He quickly adjusted his hood to cover his bloodshot eyes.

'It's just the wind,' replied Herron, as a howl went whizzing by his ears.

'No! I can hear someone screaming!'

Herron looked up at Finch and frowned as he tried to listen more carefully.

'That's the ringing in your ears again. You really must get your ears looked at.' Just then another strong gust a wind came whizzing through the carpet, blowing Herron's hood down.

AAAHHH–OOOHHH–EEEEEE! went the sound, which seemed to be coming from above their heads.

'Quick, Finch, hide!' Herron and Finch quickly disappeared in a flash back through the hole in the carpet, moving astonishingly fast. Blink and you would've missed them.

'Crash landing! OOOHHH–EEEEEE–URGH!!' screamed a little voice, as a white ball of fuzziness bounced onto the Magic Carpet, landing near to Dribble's Leap.

'Phew, that was close,' said the fuzzy white thing. She dusted herself down; she'd narrowly missed the large hole in the carpet.

'We really must get this part of the carpet repaired,' she muttered to herself, peering into the dark abyss below.

She stared silently for a moment looking into the darkness, sadness sinking into her sweet face as she sat down to catch her breath.

Two sinister red eyes quietly faded into the shadowy darkness of the abyss below her, followed by an echo.

HICCUP!

The Magic Carpet was always very peaceful at this time of day – no humans, no carpet dwellers, just the tall threads of the carpet towering majestically for miles around and the gentle vibrations of everyone snoring, It was quite comforting.

The fuzzy white thing picked herself up and headed into the forest of carpet. She hummed and whistled to herself for company as she walked through the forest. The Magic Carpet could be quite spooky in places, especially when you were on your own.

'Tum te-tum te-tum, na-na ne-ne noo-noo,' she sang, looking up at the tops of the carpet swaying gently like tall, woolly trees. The deeper into the carpet she went, the darker it got. Over the years, the carpet had collected all sorts of bits and bobs, trapping the strangest things. After twenty minutes of walking she'd passed several toe nail clippings, found four nuggets of fool's gold, which she'd stuffed into her pockets, met a grumpy old talking signpost, who'd told her to get lost when she asked for directions, and discovered two dead dust mites – they'd obviously died fighting each other as they were still in a wrestling position and covered in dust. Dust mites didn't live very long and spent most of their lives arguing with each other.

The carpet was getting thicker and thicker and there was only a small amount of light getting through to see where to walk.

'Oh, OW!' the fluff ball cried as she fell, having caught her foot on a loose thread of carpet.

THUD-THUMP! THUD-THUMP! THUD-THUMP! THUD-THUMP!

The little white fluff ball froze, her ears pricked up like a wild cat's and her fluffy back stood to attention in fright. She looked around to see where the noise was coming from, but it had stopped too quickly to tell. She couldn't make out what it was, but it felt very close; she could feel the vibrations in her hands and feet.

She waited for the sound to start again, but it didn't; just the creaking of warm floorboards and the whistle of the breeze could be heard. This deep in the Magic Carpet… alone… slightly lost… and it was getting dark.

'Panicking would probably be the next plan of action,' the fuzz ball thought calmly to herself.

Still on all fours she suddenly noticed another sound, but this was different: a very familiar sound, a comforting sound.

From a distance she could just about hear the recognizable vibrations of Bogey's tonsils, rumbling every four or five seconds. She quickly sprung to her feet and started to run in the general direction of Bogey's snoring.

'What a wonderful sound! I'll never complain about his snoring again… Hurray for Bogey's snoring… Hurray hurray!'

The snoring was getting louder, and she could also make out the faint rumblings of Smell's snoring too, just slightly out of time with Bogey's thunderous outbursts.

'I must be close,' she thought, as the familiar smell of chocolate cookies drifted through the air.

Thud-thump thud-thump THUD-THUMP THUD-THUMP! went the strange sound yet again, this time even louder and closer than before. It shook the tall threads of carpet all around, knocking things to the floor.

DOOSH! as the head of a giant half eaten Jelly Baby crashed to the floor, grinning with a sinister smile.

'AAARRRGGGHHH!' Fluff screamed in fright, as it blocked her path.

She quickly darted around the enormous baby face; she could just make out Smell and Bogey's distinctive green house through the thick threads of carpet.

THUD-THUMP THUD-THUMP THUD-THUMP THUD-THUMP!! The sound was all around her now, yet she still couldn't make out what it was.

DOOOSH! then a *WEEEEEEE!* as one of the biscuits from the morning's commotion fell out of his hiding place and scurried off into the forest.

The thick carpet opened up to reveal the familiar settings of Smell and Bogey's front yard: a neat and tidy mowed bit of carpet with a white fence fronted the little green Monopoly house that leaned slightly to the right.

The white ball of fluff dashed up to the front door and banged several times.

THUD-THUMP THUD-THUMP THUD-THUMP THUD-THUMP!! The sound was intense and all around her.

'Quick, Bogey, quick!' she screamed, looking around to see if she could make out what was making the noise. She thought for a moment she'd caught a glimpse of something staring at her from the forest.

BANG-BANG-BANG! She knocked again in a panic, stumbling into the house as the little green door slowly opened.

'Arrgghh!!' screamed Smell as he opened the door in his underpants. 'Fluff… what are you doing round?' he asked, quickly picking up a frying pan to hide his embarrassing underpants. He'd obviously just woken from his afternoon nap.

'Can't you hear the noise?' cried Fluff, peering out of the kitchen window, taking no notice of Smell's awkward situation.

'Noise… what noise?'

'That thump-thumping outside!' screamed Fluff, in a bit of a fluster.

'Oh… you mean Bogey, I thought you'd got used to his snoring?'

'No! That thumping noise outside. It's everywhere… listen!'

Smell put down the frying pan and walked over to the window, trying to wiggle his ears into the right direction to hear.

'There's no noise, Fluff,' he said confidently. Fluff listened again.

'Well, I heard it, Smelly; a horrible dull thudding sound coming from the ground.'

'Oh, you mean the engine noise.'

'Engine noise… what do you mean?' she asked, her eye suddenly catching the silliest pair of underpants she'd ever seen.

'We heard that noise this morning… we think it's some sort of engine. It's nothing to be afraid of,' he said, trying to sound brave and macho.

'Oh… you heard it this morning, did you?' Fluff said, transfixed on Smell's pants.

'Yeah, anyway you're quite safe now, Fluff, I'll protect you from any strange noises. You're in good hands here,' he bragged, putting his hands on his hips, trying to look like a superhero.

'Oh, you're my hero, Smelly. What would I do without you? We should give you a superhero name… now what could we call you?' she thinks aloud, putting her finger on her lips in deep thought.

Smell is leaning on the kitchen table beaming with pride.

'I know… we could call you Banana Pants!' She bursts into laughter at the sight of Smell in his silly underpants.

'No, wait… Strawberry Pants!' she screams, looking more closely at the fruity selection printed on Smell's underwear.

Smell quickly grabbed back the frying pan to hide behind. He was feeling very embarrassed.

Fluff had forgotten all about the strange noises outside as she clutched her stomach in pain. Her giggles had woken Bogey up too. He came downstairs and immediately burst into laughter at the sight of Smell in his fruity underpants. He'd seen them before, of course, but the fact that Fluff now knew what sort of underwear Smell wore was enough to start him off in fits of laughter.

'All right, all right then! You've had a good laugh at my pants, can we be adult about this now?' Smell sat down at the kitchen table looking slightly bored of being the butt of the joke.

Fluff and Bogey burst into louder roars of laughter.

'Oh… I'm sorry, Smelly,' Fluff replied, clutching her stomach in pain, trying to control her giggles. 'I haven't laughed for such a long time, I've been waiting for something to start me off. Thank you, Smelly, you *are* wonderful.'

Fluff hugged Smell and a big cheeky grin appeared on his face as he lapped up the affection from his favourite neighbour. Bogey raised an eyebrow as he stared at Smell enjoying every minute of Fluff's hug.

That afternoon was a great afternoon. Smell and Bogey were on form, making Fluff laugh the whole time. They told her all about

Bogey's record-breaking sneezing fit and the biscuits that didn't want to be eaten. Smell showed Fluff his entire collection of underpants – fruity pants, giraffe pants, superhero pants, monkey pants, space-ship pants, you name it.

'Where do you get them all from?' Fluff asked.

'They're presents from Aunties mainly.'

Bogey made tea and more biscuits, and this time they stayed on the plate long enough to be eaten. Smell started talking about how they had ended up in the Magic Carpet all those years ago.

'I'm so glad you two landed on the carpet,' said Fluff, tucking into her final chocolate biscuit. 'It's so much fun living next door to you two.'

'Would you like another?' asked Smell, thrusting the plate of biscuits in front of her nose.

'No, thank you, Smelly, I'd better be getting back home… I've been away for nearly four days now.'

'Yes, it has been a while. Where did you get to this time?' asked Bogey, as he started to wash up the teacups.

'I spent most of the time glued to the television set!'

'Oh… was there something good on, then?' Smell asked keenly.

'No! I was literally glued to the television in the bedroom. I was out walking the other afternoon and suddenly, *WHOOOSH!* I shot up from the carpet and ended up attached to the TV screen! For three days I was stuck.'

'Oh, yes… static electricity. You've got to be careful of that,' said Bogey, now drying up the teacups.

'The static attracts anything light and fluffy, you see,' said Fluff, looking at a puzzled Smell. 'Three days of being dazzled by a computer game called *Space Hop It* – I thought I was going to go blind.'

'How did you get down, then?' asked Smell, concerned.

'Eventually I lost my stickiness and drifted back down to the carpet… then a strong gust of wind took me, and I almost landed in Dribble's Leap!' Smell looked down at his feet at the mention of Dribble.

'You really need to start wearing some heavy shoes,' said Bogey, with one of his bright ideas. 'One of these days you'll get stuck somewhere for good.'

Fluff nodded and got up, dusting the biscuit crumbs off her lap.

'Well, I better walk you home, Fluff, it's dark outside,' said Smell, jumping to his feet.

'Thanks, Smelly, that's very thoughtful of you.'

Just then:

KNOCK–KNOCK–KNOCK! boomed the front door in a rather sinister fashion.

Smell and Bogey froze, staring at each other in fright. They never had visitors this late at night, not ever. Fluff looked at them both, puzzled; they were both frozen to the spot.

'Well… are you going to answer the door, then, boys?' Smell looked at Fluff with his mouth wide open.

'Yes, are you going to answer the door, then, Bogey?' he said.

'Me… Why have I got to answer it?'

''Coz you're the nearest to the door, that's why,' Smell said, nudging Bogey closer to the door with his elbow.

'Maybe if we leave it for a minute they'll go away,' Bogey whimpered.

'What in the Magic Carpet is wrong with you two?' exclaimed Fluff, walking over to the front door.

KNOCK–KNOCK–KNOCK!!! boomed the front door again, this time even louder than before.

'They're not going away, Boges,' said Smell apprehensively.

Fluff walked up to the door, taking a quick peak through the kitchen window, but it was too dark to see outside.

She grabbed the handle, turned it slowly, and gently opened the big green door. It squeaked, creaked and cracked as it opened. Everyone in the kitchen held their breath in anticipation.

Who or what was calling this late at night, and what did they want with Smell and Bogey?

Chapter Three

Dreams Come True

A tall hooded figure stood soaring like a giant in the tiny green doorway of Smell and Bogey's house. Fluff stared up at the gangly menacing form with no face, wishing she hadn't opened the door in the first place.

'M-may I help you?' said Fluff, in a wobbly but polite voice.

The figure stared down at the little fluff-ball, whose legs started to tremble with fear. Smell and Bogey had scrambled to the kitchen cupboard to hide. They were squabbling for space, too petrified to go anywhere near the front door.

'Will you get your smelly feet off my new slippers please, thank you!' grumbled Bogey.

'Sorry, Boges, but there isn't enough room in here for three of us,' replied Smell, fidgeting for space.

'What do you mean, three of us? There's only two of us,' Bogey said, looking puzzled.

'Me, you and that big enormous belly of yours... your belly alone takes up a whole person's space. They should charge you double when you get on a bus.'

WHACK!! went Bogey's foot on Smell's toe.

'OW!' screamed Bogey as the pain shot into his own foot.

'It serves you right for kicking me with your slippers on.'

'Oh, I'm in pain... OO-OW!' Bogey moaned, clutching at his throbbing foot.

'SSHHHH, listen!' whispered Smell, putting his ear to the crack in the cupboard door.

'Is there *anything* I can do for you?' Fluff politely asked again. She was starting to develop a crookneck.

Just then the strange creature wobbled slightly. He was dressed in a very long hooded black robe, which covered any feet he might have had and shrouded his face in darkness…

'THERE IS DANGER COMING TO THESE PARTS!!' bellowed the menacing figure. The crockery in the kitchen shuddered with the vibrations of his voice, deep and toneless.

Suddenly a dull sneeze came from the kitchen cupboard. Smell quickly grabbed Bogey's nose to silence his hooter. As he did so, Bogey's behind got the better of him and he let out what can only be described as an awkward fart.

'THERE IS DANGER COMING TO THESE PARTS!!' the lanky figure bellowed again.

'Oh, err…umm, w-what sort of danger?' whimpered little Fluff, feeling very vulnerable and alone.

'YOU MUST LEAVE THIS PLACE BEFORE IT IS TOO LATE. ALL CREATURES WILL PERISH IN THE UPRISING!!'

'What's the uprising?' whispered Smell.

'SSHHH!' said Bogey. 'I'm trying to listen.'

'Ahh – tissue!!' he sneezed again, quickly covering his face, the smell of smelly feet and farts was becoming too much for such a confined space.

'YOU MUST LEAVE THIS PLACE BEFORE IT IS TOO LATE. YOU HAVE TWENTY-FOUR HOURS UNTIL THE UPRISING!!' The lanky figure wobbled again slightly.

'Um… where should we go?' asked Fluff, bewildered.

'YOU MUST LEAVE THE MAGIC CARPET. YOU HAVE TWENTY-FOUR HOURS BEFORE THE UPRISING. YOU *HAVE* BEEN WARNED!!' And with that the strange creature disappeared in a flash.

AAAHHH – TISSUE! AAAHHH – TISSUE!! AAAHHH – TISSUE!!!

Suddenly the kitchen cupboard door burst open and out ran Smell clutching his nose in disgust. He was followed by an enormous gust of smelly wind.

WHOOOOSH!!

'Bogey, you are too much for one small cupboard! Remind me never to get in a lift with you!' He breathed a sigh of relief as fresh air drifted into his nostrils.

'SSHH, you two, listen!' cried Fluff before Bogey could argue back.

THUD–THUMP THUD–THUD–THUMP THUD–THUMP!! went the sound under their feet yet again.

That night Smell, Bogey and Fluff stayed up most of the night talking about the strange visitor and what to do. Who was the lanky creature at the door and what were the 'thud thumping' noises coming from the ground? And what were they to do? Leave the Magic Carpet indeed! Their beloved home! They couldn't take it seriously, surely? Fluff didn't feel like walking home in the dark that night, so Smell kindly offered her his bedroom. He would take the sofa downstairs in the back room. Bogey fell asleep the instant his head touched the pillow. A gentle drip of snot fell from his nostrils as the black of night quickly changed to blue of early morning.

A cool, musty breeze blew gently in through the back room window where Smell was trying to get to sleep on the most uncomfortable sofa. It was all too much for him. His feet were fidgeting under the blankets as he kept replaying the day's events over and over again in his head. Sleep was far from his mind… he'd never dreamt such excitement.

He was just starting to drift off to sleep, helped by the soothing sound of gnawing woodworms, who were busy nibbling on the dusty old piano that sat in the corner of the room, when suddenly something caught his ear.

'Smell,' whispered a very distant and muffled voice. 'Smell, hear me.'

Smell sat upright in his bed, puzzled, the bags under his eyes drooping heavily with the lack of sleep.

'Smell, hear me,' whispered the unfamiliar voice again.

Did he hear something or was he dreaming?

'I'll wake up in a minute,' he thought as he yawned the biggest yawn.

Nibble nibble nibble, went the sound of the woodworms, enjoying their musical feast. Smell flopped back into a horizontal position and covered his head with the blankets. Suddenly a gust of wind blew into the room and lifted Smell's blankets clean off him.

'Smell, hear me now... you're in big danger!' whispered the mysterious voice again. This time Smell definitely heard the cry. He sat bolt upright, his fruity banana pants on show for all to see. A number of giggles could be heard coming from the piano.

'Hello, who's that?' whispered Smell, looking around the room trying to adjust his eyes to the dark.

'Smell, listen carefully, I've come to warn ya, you gotta listen, I ain't got long.' The voice seemed to be coming from the walls of the house; it was everywhere; it sounded very chesty and wheezy.

'Who are you? Where are you? What you want with me?' Smell asked, picking up the blankets and wrapping them around him.

'I ain't got time so listen good… I'm a friend and I've gotta warn you and the others. You're all in big danger, see.'

'From the creepy creature at the door you mean?' Smell interrupted, now positively wide awake.

'That ain't the half of it. You must get everyone together first thing and leave.'

'Leave where?' Smell cried out. 'There's nowhere to go!'

'SSHH, listen, you must get……………'

The voice suddenly went silent. Not a sound could be heard.

Even the family of woodworms had stopped eating the piano to listen in on the conversation. One of them accidentally dropped a small piece of piano he'd been tucking into… *DOING!* 'SSSHHH!' The other woodworms shushed him in unison.

The backroom was still and dark, the royal blue glow of the night bounced off the shiny surfaces in the room.

'Hello? Hello?!' cried Smell, still puzzled as to where the voice was coming from. 'Hello… are you there?'

'Smell, listen carefully. I've gotta go, it's far too dangerous for me to talk, so listen up. You must all leave in the morning and head to the fireplace the other side of the Magic Carpet. Tell Ginger Bags the cat what's happened. Tell him everything. He's the only one who can help if I fail. He doesn't look it but he's clever, he'll know what to do.'

'What will happen if we stay?' asked Smell.

'YOU CAN'T STAY!! You've got less than eighteen hours left – you must tell Ginger Bags about the uprising, right? I can't tell you any more right now but you must trust me, Smell – you're all in big danger.'

'How will we find our way to the fireplace? That's hundreds of miles from here!' Smell exclaimed, realising he'd never ventured any further than the woods that surrounded their house.

'Fluff will know the way... I've gotta go now, I'll try and leave you a message at Dribble's Leap. Good luck, Smell. Remember, I'm relying on ya.'

'Don't worry, mission understood. There is one thing though... who are you?'

There was no reply...

Silence filled the back room as the royal blues of dawn slowly turned to light blues of morning. Smell lay back down on the sofa and stared at the ceiling. What excitement! What a day! He'd never dreamt of such adventure. He'd have to write this down in a book one day.

Smell eventually nodded off after playing a game of *How many noises can I hear?* The ticking of the grandfather clock in the hallway, the howling of the morning breeze through the window, the woodworm nibbling on the piano and the rumblings of Bogey's tonsils vibrating in the walls, like a faint but constant drilling. At least some one was getting a good night's sleep.

Bogey was the first to rise the next day. He'd washed the dishes, cleaned the oven, mopped the floor, made crumpets for breakfast and there was a fresh pot of tea brewing on the table. The intoxicating smell of freshly made crumpets wafted around the house as Bogey buttered one to eat. He hummed to himself as he thumbed his way through the dictionary he'd got from the kitchen dresser drawer.

'*UPRISING*… noun… rebellion, revolt, revolution, insurgence, coup, RIOT!' Bogey's face looked troubled as he read out the dictionary's definitions.

'Mornin', Bogey. Sleep all right? Something smells sweet.'

'Oh, morning, Fluff,' replied Bogey. Fluff sat down, looking at the delicious plate of crumpets oozing with butter.

'You'll make a wonderful husband one day, Bogey,' yawned Fluff, stretching her arms in the air.

'Oh, help yourself, Fluff. I made plenty for everyone. You better get one quick - things have a tendency to sprout arms and legs and leg-it in this place. Did you sleep all right?'

'Yeah, surprisingly… Smelly has a very comfy bed, I must say. I had a dream about Dribble last night. I haven't dreamt about him for ages.'

'Did you? What happened?' Bogey pried, slurping his tea.

'He came to warn me about the great danger. It felt very real.'

'Really? How did the dream end?' Bogey poured Fluff a cup of tea while munching on his third crumpet. Maple syrup dribbled down his chin.

'It went a bit weird after that. Dribble started to do some DIY around the house.'

'DIY?'

'Yes, he started drilling into the walls with an electric drill. It's funny because he hated DIY.'

'Ah, that tells me a lot, that does. That tells me you need some shelves putting up around the house, you're worried about yesterday's visitor and you still miss Dribble.'

Fluff put down her crumpet and stared at it for a moment.

'Er…more tea?' Bogey fills up her cup without waiting for a reply. 'Smelly is sleeping well considering yesterday's excitement. I'm amazed he can sleep at all after the day we had,' he said, changing the subject.

'Yeah, what did you make of it? Who was that at the door?' Fluff asked, stirring her tea.

'I've no idea... he certainly sounded strange. Didn't you get a look at his face?'

'No, it was covered up, but he did keep wobbling, as if he was dizzy or something.'

'Did you see where he went when he disappeared?' asked Bogey, stuffing his face with his fourth buttered crumpet.

'Straight up,' said Fluff. 'He moved really fast too... and he made a strange noise when he went.'

'What sort of noise?'

'I don't know... a bit like a hiccup I suppose.'

'Mornin!' yawned Smell as he burst into the kitchen in his banana pants, tripping on the kitchen rug and landing flat on his face.

'Morning, Smelly. Are you ready for breakfast? I've saved you the biggest crumpet.' Bogey had only made six crumpets and four of them had found their way into his belly. 'Would you like some tea too?'

'Er... yes please, Boges,' said Smell, looking puzzled as he picked himself up off the floor.

'How did you sleep, Fluff? Was the bed OK?'

'Yeah, you have a wonderful bed, Smelly. Thank you so much.' Fluff leaned over and gave Smell a quick peck on the cheek.

'So what's the plan for today then?' said Smell, sitting down to butter his crumpet.

'We were just talking about our strange visitor yesterday... What do you think we should do?' asked Fluff.

'I think we should forget about it,' interrupted Bogey. 'The Magic Carpet is full of weirdoes. If I ate a biscuit every time something odd happened in this place, I'd be ever so fat.'

'You are ever so fat!!' replied Smell, scoffing his crumpet. Fluff hid her grin, not wanting to upset Bogey.

'Well, I think we should call a meeting with all the locals,' said Fluff. 'What do you think, Smelly?' Suddenly Smell's eyes and mouth popped wide open in shock.

'Err... close that, please. Thank you!' said Bogey, catching a glimpse of Smell's chewed up crumpet. Smell leapt to his feet in excitement and started blurting on about something.

'Calm down and swallow before you talk,' screamed Bogey, getting the full force of Smell's splatter.

Smell sat back down and began to chew and swallow with such speed.

'We're all in great danger!' he yelled. 'We've got to leave this morning and tell Ginger Bags the cat by the fireplace – he'll know what to do! We must leave this morning, our lives depend on it!'

Fluff and Bogey looked at each other, not in the least surprised that Smell had suggested such a crazy idea.

'Well, come on then!' said Smell, 'We've got to leave before it's too late!'

'Smell, we can't possibly reach the fireplace, it's hundreds of miles away,' said Fluff.

'Where do you get your ideas from Smelly pants? That one takes the biscuit!' said Bogey, tucking into a digestive.

Smell spent the rest of that morning trying to convince Fluff and Bogey that they must try to reach Ginger Bags the cat. He told them all about the strange voice in the night and the message waiting for them at Dribble's Leap. Fluff and Bogey eventually agreed to set off on one condition. If there wasn't any message at Dribble's Leap at least they could turn back. The cat lived on the other side of the Magic Carpet, a good hundred-mile trek at least. Only Fluff had ever met him and she wasn't that sure of the route.

Smell, Bogey and Fluff left the little green Monopoly house later that morning, loaded up with supplies of biscuits, drinks and warm jumpers, with only fifteen hours before the uprising. What were they getting themselves into? Who was the mysterious voice in the night and could he be trusted?

Chapter Four

The Riddle

'I've got to stop, my feet are dropping off.'

'Will you shut up, Bogey, we've only been walking for ten minutes. We can still see the house from here!' Smell was striding ahead like a sergeant major on a mission. Bogey was waddling behind, dragging his feet in protest at all this unnecessary exercise. Bogey didn't do exercise. He'd already polished off his supply of biscuits and was wondering if the others would miss a few of theirs.

The Magic Carpet was just like a forest - tall threads of carpet towered into the air like pine trees. Some parts were thick and dense and other parts were thin and patchy. In the thickest parts it would get quite dark and creepy but in the patchy parts the midday sun would beam into every nook and cranny, showing up all the dust that settled there. A pathway meandered through the forest like a nature trail, taking them past all the sights. Past the giant head of the half eaten Jelly Baby, past the dead dust mites locked together in combat, past the grumpy signpost, who promptly told them all where to go, and quickly past the remains of a rather creepy looking creature, half maggot, half fly. It had obviously died as the fly was hatching from the maggoty shell, creating a strange half-breed that had crystallised in the sunlight. The remains were totally transparent.

'Anyone hungry yet?' asked Bogey, still far behind the other two. Fluff looked at Smell, rubbing her stomach.

'What you reckon, Smelly... shall we have a midday break? We've got quite a hike ahead of us.'

'Go on then!' said Sergeant Major Smell, surveying the area before finding a place to rest.

The midday sun wasn't as hot as usual and the three intrepid explorers managed to stay awake and eat what was left of their supplies. Bogey's backpack was almost empty, so Fluff shared out some of her portions with him.

'How do you know we're going in the right direction then, Fluff?' asked Bogey, chomping on a rather delicious plum and raisin flapjack.

'Well, I have been this way quite a few times. Dribble's Leap isn't that far, I'm sure,' she said, squinting her eyes trying to see into the thick forest that lay ahead. 'The route I haven't done is the one from Dribble's Leap to the fireplace; well, not on foot anyway.'

'Hopefully we won't need to walk that far. There won't be any message at Dribble's Leap, you'll see!' Bogey bellowed, staring at Smell.

'Aahh – tissue!' he sneezed as half of his plum and raisin flapjack shot out of his mouth and landed on Smell's sandwiches.

'Do you have to always be aiming at me when you sneeze, Boges?' Just then Fluff noticed something unusual about one of the threads of carpet behind Smell.

'Look at that thread of carpet over there. It doesn't look the same pattern as the rest of the carpet.'

The Magic Carpet had a browney, orangey red pattern to it normally, with an old-fashioned flowery design - the sort of rug you get in your grandparents' house. Smell and Bogey looked at the unusual thread towering above them. It was black and shiny with small spiky strands sticking out of it every so often.

'The carpet must have a different design nearer the centre,' said Bogey, wiping the splutter from his chops.

'No! I've seen the Magic Carpet from the air, I can never remember seeing any black in the pattern. It's all browns, oranges and reds… I'm sure of it.'

'Ooh, there's another one there, look!' said Smell. 'And another… and another!'

Four black shiny threads of carpet stood equally spaced apart amongst the oranges and browns surrounding the three travellers.

'Are you eating that cupcake?' said Bogey.

'No, you can have it, Buttercup,' said Smell.

Just then a rustling noise could be heard coming from the thick forest. Smell and Bogey froze as the threads of carpet began to move and sway.

From the darkness of the forest crawled a black scrawny creature with a blood-red eye; the other eye was missing. Just a hideous scarred eye-lid remained. The creature walked on all fours and was sniffing the ground when it suddenly stopped in its tracks and looked straight up and stared right at Smell, Bogey and Fluff, who had frozen silent…

'Oh, hello, how are you? It's not often I get visitors round these parts.' The creature stood upright on its behind legs and was making a move towards the three silent travellers. He spoke with a strained voice and even though he sounded friendly, he certainly didn't look it.

'Hello to you too. I'm Fluff from the other side of the carpet. Who are you?'

'I'm Crane. It's nice to meet you, Fluff - you're a long way from home. And who are your companions?' The creature looked up at Smell and Bogey, who were both trying to hide behind the same thread of carpet. Bogey's belly stuck out like an enormous ripe peach.

'That's Smell and that's Bogey,' pointed brave little Fluff. 'What happened to your other eye… if you don't mind me asking?' Crane's remaining eye stared intensely at her.

'Oh, I've been around for quite some time you know. I'm a flea, you know, and fleas are always getting picked on by bigger insects.'

Fluff immediately took one step back on hearing the word *flea*.

'Oh, you don't need to fear me. I'm not dangerous, not now at least. I had my day in my youth, though – oh yes! But you mellow with age, don't you, and nowadays I tend to keep out of trouble.'

In the Magic Carpet, fleas had a bad reputation for being ruthless, blood-sucking killers that liked to make war. Fluff could remember that many of Dribble's friends had been lost taking on a flea in battle.

'So what brings you out this way, Fluff?' asked Crane, walking up to Smell and Bogey.

'Oh, w-we, um, are, um, going to, um… the, um, err,' waffled Bogey as his knees wobbled from side to side.

'Really?… now that's interesting,' said Crane as he turned to look at Smell.

'We're going to Dribble's Leap,' Smell announced, finally plucking up the courage to talk.

'Dribble's Leap – hey, that's a dangerous place, Dribble's Leap!' Crane's single eye focused unnervingly on Smell.

'So why are you travelling to Dribble's Leap?'

'We're picking up a message and then we're off to talk to Ginger Bags the cat about the uprising!'

Crane's scarred eye-lid twitched as he moved closer to Smell, intrigued.

'The uprising… what's the uprising?'

'Have you not heard?' asked Fluff. 'There's something brewing, some sort of invasion and we're all in great danger!'

'Who told you that?' questioned Crane, not believing a word of it.

'We've had several visitors warning us and we only have about twelve hours left before the uprising,' said Smell.

'Who told you? Who was it?' Just then Crane stopped in his tracks and focused his eye on something in the forest. He looked and listened, transfixed. His wrinkled nose started twitching as he sniffed the air, his body colour changed from black to a deep blood red.

'What is it, Crane?' asked Fluff, looking around to see.

Crane had frozen stiff like a cat ready to pounce, his eye glued to one spot in the forest. Distant screams of strange creatures could be heard on the breeze. Smell and Bogey had huddled together behind the thread of carpet again. Even Smell was starting to doubt whether travelling this deep into the Magic Carpet was a good idea. Then Crane's eye looked up at Fluff and he began to speak in a rather nervous manner.

'What's hairy, scary and ferocious?
And will probably try and eat most of us,
Four legs at the front… and four legs at the back
And if we don't start running, we'll be under attack!
It likes to spin… the finest of thread
It has fangs in its mouth that many will dread,
It stealthily crawls, waiting for prey

And if we're not careful… we'll end up that way!'

'Hang on, hang on,' said Smell, looking baffled. 'It's hairy and ferocious and likes to eat people?'

'Yes!' Crane replied, now looking white as a sheet.

'It's got six... seven... eight legs and spins fine thread and crawls about waiting for prey?'

'Yes, you've got it!' Crane was positively trembling.

'I have no idea what you are talking about. Is there any chance you could just tell us what you mean without bursting into rhyme?'

Just then the threads of the Magic Carpet began to violently sway all around them. Crackles and snaps could be heard coming from every direction. Dust started to blow in from the forest as the ground rumbled and shook. Then the four shiny black threads of carpet that stood in front of them began to uproot from the ground and lift high into the air. Another four shiny black threads appeared behind them. Dust flew everywhere.

'AAAAAHHHHH-TISSSSUUUUE!!!' screamed Bogey as he shot backwards with the force of his sneeze.

'One, two, three, four, five, six, seven, eight legs!' counted Fluff. 'We're surrounded!'

'By what?' cried Smell.

'SPI-DER!!!! AAAAHHHHH!!!!'
screamed Bogey as one of the black hairy legs
grabbed his bulging waist and elevated him
high into the air, tightening its grip the higher
they went.

The spider let out an almighty clattering
roar, a roar like you've never heard before –
half roar, half scream.

Fluff and Crane ran as fast as they could
away from the enormous creature that towered
above them like a huge mechanical bulldozer.

'Run, Smell, quickly! Run!!' yelled Fluff,
looking round to see another dangly leg
heading straight for him.

'AAAAHHHHH!!!!' Smell was too slow. The black spindly leg grabbed him and spun him around and around, tightening its grip as Smell hurtled into the air. Another shuddering scream echoed throughout the Magic Carpet.

'SMELL!' screamed Fluff as she turned back towards the terrifying beast. Drool oozed and dribbled down from the pointed fangs that Smell and Bogey were heading straight towards.

Fluff jumped onto one of the hairy legs and tried to bite with all of her mite, but the spider's leg just flipped her up into the air with a flash. She disappeared over the tops of the carpet.

'AAAAHHHHH... HELP!!!!' screamed Smell as he got closer and closer to the spider's jaws. He could see beyond the two large fangs and into the awful hideous mouth, where lots of tiny fangs dripped acidic mucus ready to dissolve its prey.

'SMELLY!!!' screamed Bogey as he saw the giant mouth open and close over Smell's tiny body… and then he was gone…

Meanwhile, Crane had hidden in a thick part of carpet. He was watching the whole thing unfold with his beady bloodshot eye.

'Help me!' came a voice from above. Crane looked up to see Fluff clinging to the tops of the carpet. She was stuck and wriggling to get free. Crane grabbed hold of the carpet thread and tugged hard. She came loose and was free for a moment but the commotion from the spider had caused such a draft that she continued to float on the breeze.

Suddenly the spider's grip on Bogey loosened and he fell to the floor with a dusty bump. He quickly ran as fast as he could into the shade of the carpet to hide. The spider was sniffing the air and looking rather puzzled.

'Over here!' cried Crane as he waved Bogey over to his hiding place. The breeze was blustering all around them blowing up dust and debris. 'What happened to Smell?' Crane enquired.

'The spider… he got him, I think he got him,' whimpered Bogey, ducking from a low flying toenail clipping that had caught the breeze.

'We've gotta run, Bogey, the spider won't stop until he's had his fill. Follow me!' said Crane.

'No!!' yelled Bogey. 'I'm not leaving!'

'You must, it's too dangerous! You can't fight a spider. What you gonna do, sneeze on him?!'

Just then, Bogey noticed the spider had opened his mouth wide and looked rather uncomfortable. The menacing hairy creature towered above them like a giant statue, his huge pointy fangs gleamed in the sunlight, eight eyes, two large and six smaller ones twitched at every movement. There were spider legs all over the place, spindly, hairy and black.

'Look!' Bogey pointed. 'Can spiders smell?' he asked Crane.

'Um… yes… I think so. Why?'

The spider was shaking his head from side to side and making an awful clicking and screaming noise. Slimy mucus was flying in all directions from its mouth, like one of those dogs that dribbles everywhere. Then he stopped, looked up into the sky and paused… and then…

'AAAAAHHHHH   TISSSSUE!!!!!' screamed the spider in a window-shatteringly loud sneeze. The ground shook with the vibration. Out flew every bit of gooey mucus, slimy dribble and oily splatter. One bit hit Bogey slap in the face.

'AAHHH get it off me, AAHHH!' he screamed jumping frantically up and down.

'AAAAAHHHHH   TISSSSUE!!!!!' the spider screamed again, this time blowing Fluff back down to the ground. Bogey quickly ran over to grab her. She was just as likely to blow off again.

'AAAAAHHHHH TISSSSUE!!!!!'

'OOOOOHHHHH… Out the way, out the way!!!' came a familiar voice.

Bogey, Fluff and Crane looked up to see a soggy looking face plummeting toward them...

'DUCK!' screamed the voice as a slimy ball of mucus shot out of the spider's mouth and landed at their feet.

'Smelly, you're safe! Oh, you're safe!' cried Fluff as she fussed over him, getting covered in mucus.

'I thought you were a goner,' said Bogey as he handed Smell a hanky to wipe off the slime from his face.

The spider was clearly in distress, coughing and spitting wildly. The smell of Smell had been too intense. He turned around and made his way back into the depths of the carpet, dribbling and whining, legs clicking as he went.

'Thank goodness you're safe, Smelly. Are you hurt?' asked Fluff, still wiping his face.

'No, I'm fine, I managed to dodge the spider's teeth and hide until... well, something must have irritated him.'

'That'd be you, you wally! Have you smelt yourself recently?' said Bogey, blowing his nose with his hanky. As he took the hanky away from his nose it became apparent that it had made things worse. Oozing down from Bogey's nose was a cascade of spider's dribble; it looked like a slimy stalactite dangling from his hooter.

'I'm not smelly - that's all this spider mucus I'm covered in,' said Smell, trying to convince everyone he didn't always smell that bad.

Just then from deep within the Magic Carpet came an enormous ferocious roar. It pierced the late afternoon sky with a shuddery shrill.

'It's Fangs again, the spider!' said Crane, looking all around with his one beady eye.

'We must get moving - he could be coming back any minute!'

Smell, Bogey, Fluff and Crane cleaned themselves up, got their stuff together and trekked off into the carpet. Deeper and deeper into the thick forest they went. They hadn't been going more than five minutes when they came to a clearing in the carpet. The threads weren't worn out - they were matted together and flattened with hardened grime.

'This must be Dribble's Leap!' exclaimed Bogey in delight. He'd walked more than he'd ever walked in his life already and was ready to put his feet up.

Fluff looked up into the sky and sniffed the air.

'What is it, Fluff?' asked Smell.

'This isn't Dribble's Leap. Can't you feel the change in pressure? There's a wind blowing in with a lot of force behind it. I can sense the pressure is really strong.'

The boys looked around them, huddling together for protection.

'Ah, that's ya imagination, Fluff. The deeper ya go into the carpet, the more your mind plays tricks on ya,' said Crane, stretching his back legs. They clicked and creaked with age.

Smell had leaned onto a clump of matted carpet to rest a minute, but when he went to move his hand away, it had stuck fast.

'Ah, I'm stuck!' he said, pulling his hand with his other one to set it free.

'Will you just stay out of trouble for one moment!' said Bogey.

'What? I can't help it if my hands stuck!'

'You're always getting into trouble, I've never known such a…'

'Boys! Oh boys, I think you should hold on tight to something…' said Fluff, still looking up into the air. All the white fluffy hairs on her back were standing up on end. Crane could sense something too as he cowered away into the cover of the carpet.

'What? What is it, Fluff?'

Those were Bogey's famous last words. For what was about to unfold only helped confirm to Smell that the greatest of adventures did indeed happen if you went looking for them…

Chapter Five

MILKSHAKE!

WHOOOSH – BANG!! went the spare bedroom door as it flung open to the sound of five screaming and excitable human children. They piled into the room where the Magic Carpet lay, running around like headless chickens, wild and excited. There were children jumping up and down on the old feather bed, children climbing onto shelves, dropping sweet wrappers and rolling on the Magic Carpet in their brand new trainers.

'Where's my old Action Man?' screamed one spotty eleven year old as he climbed a dusty shelf and rummaged through hundreds of old toys from birthdays and Christmases gone by.

'Ah ha, I've got him!' yelled another, dark haired boy. He was throwing the figure high into the air and deliberately not catching him. The Action Man plummeted to the floor.

'Oi!' screamed the spotty one. 'That's an eagle eyed Action Man. It's antique and it's my big brother's, so leave off, will ya!'

The dark haired boy had joined the rest of the boys on the old feather bed to see who could jump the highest. He lobbed the action hero onto the floor.

Boing – Boing, Thud – Thump, Doing – Doing! went the springs in the old bed. A thick dust cloud gathered pace across the spare room.

'Oi yous lot, calm down and less of the noise!' came a mumsy voice from downstairs.

CRASH! went an enormous baked bean tin full of pencil crayons and felt-tipped pens. They shot across the room in every direction.

'Liam!! Now that's enough! I'm warning you, I won't say it again. Now calm down!'

The boys had just come back from celebrating the spotty one's birthday. Liam was eleven today and had invited all his closest mates round for birthday cake. They were swigging the last drops of their 'Go-Large' sized drinks and milkshakes, which had obviously made them all hyper. The dust was getting thicker and thicker - you could hardly see through it! The boys were bouncing higher and higher on the old bed and the noise level had peaked to *'Driving mum up the wall level'* when suddenly the inevitable happened...

BANG – WHOOSH – AAAHHH!!! The legs of the old bed gave way and five manic eleven year olds went flying through the air, milkshakes and all. They landed in a heap on the Magic Carpet followed by a splish and a splosh as the dregs of milkshake sprayed over the carpet.

'Right, that's it, out of there now and get down here. I've got birthday cake!' came the angry mumsy cry from downstairs.

'Birthday cake', being the magic words for most eleven year old boys, had an equally magical effect... not a boy in sight.

The dust started to settle in the spare room. Things had stopped wobbling from the commotion and all that remained were a few pink blobs of milkshake splattered over the Magic Carpet...

'What, Fluff, what is it?' cried Bogey.

'Bogey, duck right now!' screamed Smell. His hand was still stuck to the manky bit of Magic Carpet and he could see what was heading Bogey's way. Fluff had taken cover and Crane was nowhere to be seen.

Bogey turned around to see what Smell was looking at and then...

SPLOOOOOSSSHHH!!!!!!!

A gallon or more of the stickiest, gooiest pink milkshake covered poor old Bogey from head to toe. Strawberry milkshake went everywhere, in his ears, up his nose, in his pockets and down his pants.

'Help, I can't breathe!' came a muffled cry from underneath the fat pink wobbling blob. Fluff and Smell run to his rescue, trying to make a hole for his mouth. They giggled to themselves as they rummaged around trying to find his mouth and eyes.

'Oh, you think it's funny do you?' screamed Bogey, who now resembled a giant pink talking marshmallow with eyes. He wobbled around trying to maintain his balance.

'Why am I always getting covered in it?' he moaned.

'I'm fed up with this! I haven't eaten for hours, my legs are aching, I'm covered in slime and I want to go home!'

'I don't know why you're complaining, Boges. Have you tasted what you're covered in?' said Smell licking his lips at the sight of a giant milkshake-man standing before him. His belly rumbled.

Bogey's tongue tried a sample from around his lips…

'MILKSHAKE!! I'm covered in strawberry milkshake, my favourite milkshake. Oh boy, this must be what heaven is like for sure!'

Bogey started slurping and scooping all the extra thick milkshake he could gather into his mouth as he danced around the carpet in delight. Smell and Fluff had started to eye up Bogey's pink limbs as well. He'd suddenly become very edible.

The Magic Carpet had started to get dark and cool by the time they had cleaned up Bogey. Just his feet remained pink from the sticky milkshake. Bogey said it was emergency supplies for when he got hungry later.

His belly looked a lot fatter than normal; it was really bulging and gurgling with all the sugariness. Fluff and Smell had also tucked into the tasty windfall. The friends were telling stories as they sat and relaxed around a flickering campfire deep in the Magic Carpet.

'There's no such thing as ghosts!' said Bogey, rubbing his enormous belly.

'Ooh, I feel sick,' said Fluff, as she lay down trying to find more room in her stomach for all the milkshake she'd consumed.

'How can you say that, Boges? You've never seen one.'

'Exactly!' said Bogey. Smell, Bogey and Fluff rested their weary bodies as the campfire crackled. Such an exciting day, bellies full and minds racing with thoughts, but no one had realised that someone was missing…

Bogey's snoring could be heard for miles around in the Magic Carpet that night. The tall milkshake covered threads of carpet wobbled with the vibrations. He lay on his back with his legs in the air, the only way he could get comfy with such a full belly. Smell was staring into the fire; he couldn't sleep and felt it only right to keep a look out while Fluff was resting. Her pretty face shimmered in the firelight as her ears and nose twitched every so often.

The dead of night brought a bitter chill to the air. The Magic Carpet was in the spare room of Liam's house and the heating was very rarely put on. The campfire had burnt out to a dull molten glow. Smell had now joined the slumber party, dribbling contently like a baby, teeth nattering and clattering each time he breathed in.

Off in the distance, in the darkness, something moved silently amongst the threads.

Two blood-red-eyes stared fixed on the sleeping party, then another two eyes appeared. Rustling could be heard coming from the forest and then what sounded like a hiccup… Then something else moved into view. Strange little black creatures started to swarm in the forest, sniffing the ground as they scurried in the shadows; the two red beady eyes retreated into the dark. Things were on the move in the dead of night. Creepy crawlies with tiny antennas wriggling on their heads swarmed towards Smell, Bogey and Fluff. Closer and closer, hundreds and hundreds of creatures engulfed the campsite, following each other with military precision.

They seemed to take a shine to Bogey, ignoring Smell and Fluff as they crawled all over him. In his ears they crawled, over his belly they crawled, in-between his toes they crawled and even down his pants they crawled.

'Aaaahhhh!! Bogey, wake up!' screamed Fluff as she woke up with a jolt, which in turn woke Smell. Bogey still lay there fast asleep snoring his head off, covered in crawly creatures.

'Blur-cough-splutter!' he choked as he finally woke up, almost swallowing a number of the creatures that had gathered around his mouth.

'Ahh! Get them off! Get them off me!' he shouted, jumping to his feet.

'Ants, you're covered in ants, Boges. Quick, shake them off, they're everywhere!' yelled Smell as Bogey danced up and down trying to clear off the swarming blighters from his belly.

Then a number of the ants piled on top of each other forming a tower, then a bigger ant climbed to the top of the tower.

'A hum...' The hunky ant cleared his throat.

'Why, hello,' he remarked as his muscles gleamed in the moonlight. He had the perfect ant physique and a very noble gaze, although his nose was rather big for his head; it stuck out a little bit too much. It was so big he couldn't see straight without tilting his head.

'Who?' said Bogey, stunned and still half asleep.

'I do apologise most awfully for my men, they do get terribly enthusiastic. They're trained to be the best you see, no stopping them once they're orf.'

'Hello there,' said Fluff as she did what can only be described as a half curtsey out of politeness. The noble ant turned to Fluff with a twinkle in his eye. He beamed with affection.

'Oh, my dear, how rude of me, allow me to introduce myself. My name is Lord Itch. I serve and defend the Queen and command all her loyal servants.' He pointed to the hundreds of ants that had gathered. They all saluted and stamped their feet in unison.

'It's very nice to meet you. Do you all live round here?' inquired Fluff, putting on a rather posh voice.

'Ah, alas, I can't disclose that information, I'm afraid. Breach of security and all that, you understand. The Queen's safety is paramount you know.'

'Oh, of course,' said Fluff, staring at his enormous hooter.

Smell, Bogey, Fluff, Lord Itch and his hundred strong men sat around the dying camp fire until the early hours singing ant songs and sharing stories, although every time Fluff asked Lord Itch a question she got the same response. *'I can't disclose that information, I'm afraid. Breach of security, you understand?'*

'Well, it's been fascinating learning about ants!' yawned Smell, bored with the conversation.

'Yes, but you haven't told me what a fine body of men such as yourselves are doing this deep in the Magic Carpet. It's not for the faint hearted, you know,' replied Lord Itch, sounding positively regal.

'We're going to talk to Ginger Bags the cat,' said Smell.

'Er, we're going to Dribble's Leap!' Bogey butted in.

Fluff explained to Lord Itch the strange noises, the tall hooded figure at the door and the warning Smell had had in the middle of the night.

'Well dingle me tomcats,' exclaimed Lord Itch, looking puzzled. 'You are in a spot of bother. I don't like the sound of all that lot at all.'

'Can you help us at all?' asked Bogey, looking exhausted from lack of sleep.

'Yes! I shall! It sounds like you need a military mind on board!'

Lord Itch turned to his men, who had all fallen asleep, and started to rally the troops.

'Men, if our gallant friends are correct, we could all be in grave danger, the Queen included!'

A gasp echoed through the troops.

'I will accompany our new friends on their noble mission and you, my fine men, shall head back to H.Q. and protect the Queen. Her safety is paramount!'

'HURRAHHH!!!!!' cheered the men, stamping their feet in approval.

By daybreak the next morning, Lord Itch had disbanded his men back to H.Q. and planned a strategic offensive, giving it the name 'Operation Ginger Storm'. The rest of the clan had fallen back to sleep in the hope of getting some rest before any more excitement.

'Right, come on men, rise and shine! There's work to be done!' bellowed Lord Itch as he woke up the camp.

'Aahhh, w-what time is it?' asked Bogey, his eyes refusing to open.

'0500 hours and time we were orf!' announced Lord Itch, packing up the essentials.

'Oh, that's OK then, I thought it was early.'

'That's five o'clock in the morning, Bogey,' said Fluff, trying to find the energy to get herself up.

'F-five o'clock in the morning!!!' yelled Bogey, which woke Smell up from his deep slumber. He was having a great dream about being a sergeant in the army.

Suddenly an almighty roar bellowed with intense ferocity above the thread tops and two giant silvery fangs appeared out of nowhere, dripping with a toxic slime. The whole carpet shook with fear. The enormous roar and deafening screams came from *Fangs*, the hungry and very grumpy spider.

'Quick, you lot, move it!!' came a familiar voice.

'Crane, where have you been?' said Fluff, jumping to her feet. Two enormous fangs were heading her way.

'Quick, run. Follow me!' Crane screamed as Fangs' spindly legs clambered into the opening of the Magic Carpet. Bogey ducked just in time to avoid being sliced in two by the giant molars…

They ran for miles in the morning light through the thick forest of carpet.

'Ow!' screamed Bogey as he clipped his foot, nearly stumbling to the floor. 'I wanna go home and tidy the kitchen… and make some biscuits… and polish the kettle and iron the dishes and empty the bins!' he muttered to himself, trying to focus on positive things he loved. He was struggling to keep up with the others.

'Stop… please stop, I can't run anymore!' he yelled, dripping wet with sweat from all the exercise.

'Look over there!' pointed Smell. 'There's a doorway we can hide in.' Smell had spotted a large cave-like opening. It looked like an entrance that had been woven into the carpet. It wasn't the most inviting, but given the choice… A spooky uninviting cave or being eaten alive by a ferocious giant spider... Which would you choose?

Smell, Bogey and Fluff introduced Lord Itch to Crane as they gingerly made their way through the giant arched doorway of the cave. Deeper and deeper they went. It was covered from floor to ceiling in a white woven sticky thread. The deeper they went, the darker the cave got.

'At least we've got away from the awful spider,' said Smell, trying to put a positive thought into the air.

'Yeah, and now we're trapped in a sticky cave!' replied Bogey.

'Nice plan, Smelly pants!'

'Shush, you two!' said Fluff, squinting her eyes to make out what was ahead.

'Is that light I can see at the end of the tunnel?'

'Hang on, I'll get my night-vision spectacles out. They'll soon tell us what's up ahead, my dear.' Lord Itch rummaged around his waistcoat pocket.

'Ah yes, here we go, now then… It seems to be another doorway.'

'It's the way out, I know it!' said Smell bounding ahead like an excited puppy.

The doorway led to a giant catacomb with a number of routes leading off in different directions.

'Oh, brilliant, Smelly, you've found an enormous sticky maze!' cried Bogey, getting one of his feet stuck on the tacky ground.

'It's got to lead out eventually. Can't you feel the breeze blowing ahead? I read about this once – if you follow the breeze, you'll reach the end of the tunnel, I'm sure,' said Smell.

'It's better than going back the way we came. I don't fancy bumping into Fangs again,' moaned Crane, bent over and rubbing his back.

The intrepid explorers picked up their things and edged tentatively ahead into one of the tunnels. The deeper they went, the more the tunnels would split off and divide into even more passageways. After ten minutes there were tunnels everywhere and the width was narrowing.

'I don't like this much,' Bogey mumbled, looking around at all the strange-cocooned figures that lined each corridor.

'Are they people?' asked Fluff, having a closer look.

'They can't be, they're made from the same stuff the walls are made from,' said Smell as he fondled one of the ghostly looking figures.

AAAAAHHHHHH-TISSSSUUUEEEE!!!!

'AAAAHHHHHH!!!!' Smell screamed, as the figure he'd been fondling suddenly came to life with an almighty sneeze.

A frenzied commotion broke out in the rapidly narrowing tunnel until a muffled little voice could be heard.

'Don't hurt me, please don't hurt me.'

'Stop panicking and listen,' cried Fluff as she went over to the little white figure that trembled with fear.

'It's all right, we won't hurt, are you all right?'

AAAAHHHHHH-TISSSSSUEEEE!!!!
screamed the little creature, splattering Fluff in
the face with spray. Two solemn eyes peered
from behind the white masked face. His arms
were bound behind his back like a straitjacket
as he quivered in fright. He was rooted to the
spot.

'Are you OK?' asked Smell as he moved
closer.

'Well, I've been better thanks,' replied the
trembling little voice.

'I'm Smell, what's your name? Are you a
ghost?'

'My name's Crumb and, no, I'm not a
ghost… I've been trapped like this for ages,
see.'

'Oh, you poor thing,' said Fluff as she moved in to help unravel him.

AAAAHHHHH-TISSSSUUUUEEEE!!!!
splattered Crumb again. Everyone ducked together, avoiding the snotty shower.

'I'm sorry about this… I'm allergic to dust, see. You must be fluff?'

'Yes, that's right. How did you know my name?'

'Oh, I didn't, I'm just allergic to dust and fluff and stuff.'

Smell, Bogey and Lord Itch helped unravel little Crumb from the stringy threads that had trapped him for so long. Underneath the cocooned woven shell was a handsome beady-eyed crumb, probably of the chocolate digestive variety. Half of his body was digestive biscuit and the other was covered in dark chocolate. He had a very friendly smile but months of being cocooned had taken its toll – his face was drawn and stressed with dark bags under his eyes.

'I don't suppose you know the way out of here?' enquired Crane, who towered over Crumb.

'Err, yes I think I can remember. It's the way you came in. You can't get out the other way. That leads to Fangs' nest.

'Fangs!!' cried Bogey.

'Yes, this is his lair. Didn't you know?'

'No, we were trying to get away from him,' said Fluff, not wanting to get too close in case she caused another sneezy outburst.

SSSCCCCRRRREEEEAAAACCCHHH!!!!

Suddenly from behind Crumb's head appeared the familiar fangs of Fangs' teeth as he pounced onto the group from nowhere. Crane jumped out of the way in a flash, while the rest of the group started to run for their lives.

'Quick yous lot, follow me!' cried Crumb as he started to run.

Fangs was wriggling to get free; he'd got one of his legs stuck in his own sticky web.

'We must run faster, people!' demanded Lord Itch, who was way out in front. Looking back he could see Fangs had gotten free and was thundering closer and closer.

'I don't know which way it is!' cried little Crumb, puzzled by so many tunnels forking ahead.

'Look there!' screamed Fluff.

'What are those footprints?'

'They're my footprints!' announced Bogey, pointing at the dinky pink footsteps that covered the tunnel floor.

Bogey's milkshake-covered feet had mapped out the way out, on the way in.

'Follow those footshakes!!!' screamed Smell, as Fangs appeared right behind Fluff. Toxic dribble poured from his teeth. His legs blocked every other exit. The beginning of the maze was in sight. Smell could feel the fresh breeze as the light poured into the tunnel up ahead. Even though the six ran like they'd never ran before, Fangs the spider was closing in on them fast. They could not out-run him. Even if they did make it out of the lair, they'd be easy prey out in the open. As Smell reached the opening of the maze, he looked back to see his friends screaming as they ran. The spider towering above them suddenly let out a deafening scream as he opened his mouth wide and lunged forward with all of his might.

Chapter Six

The Love Bubble

'Jump onto my back!' yelled Crane as he reached the entrance to the spider's lair. The daylight was blinding after being trapped in the dark tunnels of the maze.

'May I ask what you have in mind?' said Lord Itch, out of breath and puzzled by Crane's announcement.

'I can jump very fast. If you all grab on, I think we can escape!'

'Are you sure, Crane? There's a lot of us,' said Fluff, concerned for Crane's aging body. He wasn't exactly young and agile any more.

'There's no time to discuss it, just grab on now if you're coming. I'm not hanging around here!'

Smell grabbed onto one leg and Bogey another. Fluff and Crumb climbed onto Crane's back and Lord Itch clasped his hands around Crane's waist. Crane lowered himself into a crouching position, his legs creaked and cracked as he tensed his muscles.

'You better get a move on, Crane. Here comes Fangs!' Smell averted his eyes as Fangs shrieked an enormous scream as he reached the lair entrance.

'I don't think this is going to work, guys.' Crumb trembled as he stared up at Fangs towering above him, drops of spider dribble dripping and splashing all around like rain.

SCCCRREEEEAAAAKKKK!!!! roared Fangs as he lunged forward to devour his prey… Suddenly with an almighty *TWANG!* Crane's legs released all the coiled up energy within his muscles and with an amazing *WHOOOSH!!!!* the six hurtled up into the air like a rocket, up, up and away from the spider.

The wind blew intensely as they shot up vertically with such enormous speed. Everyone held on for dear life. Crane had streamlined his body to achieve more lift. They were free from the spider!

The Magic Carpet looked so far away as they started to lose momentum. Everything looked so small. Even the huge spider looking up at them looked tiny from way up here. For a moment everyone had a brief sense of elation. They were flying – what a sensation of total freedom! Even Bogey felt a moment of excitement as the six flew like birds on the breeze. Smell loved every minute of it…

'What a great adventure,' he thought to himself.

'Now hold on tight, this is the tricky bit. Landing is always the hardest part!' yelled Crane as the flying mass of bodies started to slow down.

'Eh?' screamed Crumb, who could barely hear a thing with the rushing wind blowing in his ears.

'I say, what is the form for landing, old chap?' enquired Lord Itch, trying to sound cool and calm but secretly quite concerned at the prospect of plummeting to the ground.

'There isn't one, you just fall and hope you land back on your feet!' yelled Crane, eyeing up a landing site below.

'OOOH, we're gonna die, I know it!' cried Crumb, looking as white as he did when he was wrapped up in spider-web.

As the six lost momentum and started to head back down to Earth, Smell was the first to notice a rather worrying thing…

'Err… I don't want to alarm anyone but we seem to be heading straight back to where we came from!'

'AAAAAAHHHHHHHHHH!!!!!' everyone screamed as they hurtled straight back towards Fangs the spider. He'd laid out a dining table and chairs and was sharpening his fangs ready for the incoming feast.

The elation of flying had quickly turned to panic.

'To think I could've been finishing the ironing if I'd stayed at home,' Bogey moaned.

Fangs opened wide, his two big molars glistened in the daylight, sharp, pointy and very deadly. Suddenly out of nowhere a clear spherical ball appeared below them, then another and another. Lots of bubbles blew in on the wind.

'What are they?' cried Crumb.

'Oh, wow, they're Love Bubbles. Quick, steer us into one, Crane, we might be able to ride one!' screamed Fluff, who'd seen them before.

Crane wiggled and twitched and managed to steer into the path of one of the larger bubbles. Then, with a strange muffled flop, the group fell right into the bubble.

'Woah, this is weird. How are we doing this?' Crumb was staring right at Fangs below but instead of falling toward him they were floating in mid air.

'It's a Love Bubble. You can ride the swells of air like on a surf board,' said Fluff.

'A Love… Bubble?' Crane questioned.

'Well, I call them Love Bubbles; they're great fun. But you must think positive happy thoughts or you'll drift back down to the ground. They feed off positive energy.'

'I've never heard such a load of rubbish!' Crane wasn't buying it at all and immediately the Love Bubble lost its float and started to fall out of the sky toward Fangs.

'AAAAHHHHHH, think happy, think positive!!!' everyone screamed at Crane.

'Hang on, hang on, I'm not in the zone to think happy… wait a minute.' Crane focused his one bloodshot eye, his hands pressing on his temples. Suddenly the Love Bubble shot up again, with good pace too.

'Ooh… wait… I didn't like that!' Crumb was clutching his stomach and looking very green. His belly gurgled and rumbled. The sudden change of direction obviously didn't agree with Crumb's tummy.

'He's gonna go!' yelled Smell, pointing at Crumb's belly. He was bent over with one hand on his stomach and the other trying to steady himself against the sides of the bubble wall.

Immediately, the bubble fell back toward the Magic Carpet. Everyone screamed and panicked. A right commotion broke out. Crane shouted at Crumb, Smell yelled at Crane for shouting at Crumb, Lord Itch shouted at Smell for shouting at Crane for shouting at Crumb… and so on and so on. All this turmoil just made the Love Bubble fall faster and faster out of the sky.

'STOP IT… STOP IT NOW!!!' yelled Fluff in a rare display of aggression – a truly thunderous outburst. Even the sides of the bubble wall wobbled with the force of her voice.

'THINK HAPPY THOUGHTS OR ELSE WE'RE ALL DOOMED! NOW WHAT'S IT GONNA BE?' Fluff's face had gone bright pink and her eyes were bulging too. Bogey looked to see if steam was coming out of her ears. Everyone just stopped and looked at Fluff in amazement. Nobody had ever seen her so angry before and it was quite amusing to see this sweet little fluffy ball of fuzziness suddenly erupt into a wild monster.

Bogey chuckled and immediately farted in a moment of weakness. Smell looked up at Bogey in shock and then burst out laughing. Bogey roared with laughter back. Then Lord Itch's enormous nose got a whiff of Bogey's fart. He yelled at Bogey in disgust, trying not to giggle as he covered his face. Then Crumb started laughing at Lord Itch.

'There's no escape for you with that enormous hooter on ya face!' he blurted out. That in turn started Crane off as he too joined in with the giggle attack. Fluff stared at the silly boys, wriggling around on their backs giggling away, trapped in the pongy bubble, floating above the Magic Carpet seconds from certain death. And then...

Fluff too burst out into tears of laughter, joining the boys in hysterics... What a sight.

The Love Bubble immediately shot back up into the air and glided gracefully over the Magic Carpet to the disappointment of Fangs below. The afternoon sunshine reflected off the bubble causing sprays of colour to leap out from the elegant sphere. Blues, reds, violets and greens filled the sky. What a way to travel.

'Look, there's our house!' cried Smell, amazed to see the quaint little green Monopoly house poking out from the woolly forest.

'We haven't got very far, have we?'

'Things always look nearer from the air. Look, there's Dribble's Leap over there!' pointed Fluff, who'd had plenty of experience of flying.

'Where?' cried Smell.

'Wow, we're almost there, Boges. Look.' He pointed at the barren opening in the middle of the Magic Carpet. They were very high up now. You could see for miles and miles.

Then into view came a very strange looking object, a fluffy star-shaped floaty thing that came drifting past the bubble.

'I say… what is it, Fluff? Have you ever seen such a thing?' said Lord Itch, squinting hard to focus.

'I don't know, but it looks sharp. We'd better steer away from it, it could pop the bubble.'

'It's the seed of a dandelion. It's perfectly harmless,' announced Crane, who'd been busy scouring the Magic Carpet below.

Suddenly something very fast flew past the Love Bubble.

WHOOOOSH!!!! it went, causing the bubble to sway violently from side to side.

'WOAH! Did you see that?' said Smell.

'What was it, Smelly?' asked Fluff, looking down through the transparent floor they were standing on.

'I don't know but it was travelling very fast and looked very sharp and pointed to me.'

WHOOOOSH!!!! went another one, this time not as near to the bubble but it still caused turbulence.

'We've got to climb higher!' cried Crumb, looking a greeny shade of white.

Back down on terra firma Herron and Finch were having a whale of a time close to Dribble's Leap. Finch had found his old catapult and Herron was showing him how good a shot he was.

'Here we go… this is going to be a goodun. Now watch this!' Herron bragged as he stretched the elastic of the catapult tightly back to his shoulder. It creaked and twanged with the tension.

PING… WHOOOOSH! Herron and Finch watched the contents of the catapult zoom into the air.

'OOOHHHH, that were so close, you almost had that one then… *Hiccup!* My go, my go!' Finch said, excitedly grabbing the catapult form Herron.

'Now aim with your eyes this time. You've got to squint and aim for the middle of the bubbles,' said Herron. They were playing target practice with the Love Bubbles above, not knowing that one of them contained Smell, Bogey and the rest of the gang.

Finch pulled the elastic back as far as he could manage, squinted with one eye and then…
HICCUP… PRANG… WHISSSHHH!!!

The contents of the catapult went whizzing out of control, bounced on the floor nearly taking Herron's head off and landed somewhere in the forest.

'OI!' came a yell from the Magic Carpet.

Finch stood gormless and looked at Herron, the elastic of the catapult wrapped around his spindly arm.

'You really are the centre of the dim universe, aren't you, Finch!'

'Thanks,' Finch replied, taking Herron's insult as a compliment.

Herron picked up the catapult, loaded it with shot and stretched tightly, aiming at one of the bigger bubbles.

'Now watch and learn… this is how the professionals do it, Finchy-boy!'

WHOOOOOSHHH!!!! Herron let go. The shot zoomed into the sky and popped one of the largest bubbles.

BOOM!!! The bubble burst with an enormous sub-sonic bang.

'Wow, that was a loud one! Did you see that?' Herron sniggered like a little school kid in the playground.

'Eh… what… eh, I can't hear anything!' cried Finch, wiggling his ears, trying to restore the sound.

'Will you keep it down per-lease!' came an annoyed voice from within the forest of carpet. Droplets of debris fell to the ground around their feet. Herron chuckled to himself as Finch yanked on his ears hoping the sound would come back.

High up in the atmosphere, panic had broken out in one of the Love Bubbles. Smell and Bogey's bubble had been blown off course by the enormous explosion and the vibrations had made everyone dizzy.

'Oh, my head… I haven't felt this bad since I sniffed Smell's sock drawer and fainted with the deadly whiff,' said Bogey, steadying his head. Smell looked at Bogey but was far more interested in stopping the vibrations in his head than bothering to answer back.

'What was that? said Crumb, looking at Lord Itch.

'I don't know old chap, but we'd be safer back on old terra firma if you ask me.'

'I rather be on the ground, thanks!' said Crumb, not realising terra firma *was* the ground.

'What about the spider!' Crane cried. He too was looking a bit peaky.

'What's that enormous orange lump over there, Fluff?' asked Crumb, who was now looking greener than a bowling lawn.

'Oh, wow! That's old Ginger Bags. He's asleep look.' The sphere lifted higher again until almost all of the Magic Carpet had come into view.

'How do we steer this thing?' asked Smell, pushing on the sides of the bubble.

'We must make it to Ginger Bags! We've got to tell him about the uprising!'

Immediately the bubble lost its lift and with a sudden jolt started to lose altitude.

'What did you do?' said Bogey, looking slightly unnerved.

'Who's not thinking happy thoughts?' Fluff looked around at the boys. No one responded.

The transparent sphere started to fall back toward the carpet. Fluff started to push on one side of the bubble to influence its direction. Smell pushed on the other as the bubble picked up speed. Bogey put his hands on his ears hoping this was all a dream and Crumb, Lord Itch and even the stern, cold-hearted Crane huddled together in one corner of the Love Bubble and hoped for a soft landing.

'I'd hold on tight if I were you!' screamed Crane.

As the Love Bubble hurtled out of control toward the Magic Carpet, Fluff was thinking of every happy thought she could imagine. The happy times with Dribble before he'd disappeared, the fun picnics and romantic evenings by the fire on cold winter's evenings and the fun and silly times she'd spent with Smell and Bogey.

'Bogey, if there was ever an appropriate moment to let one off... now is that time!' said Fluff. Even she couldn't believe she'd witnessed herself saying such un-lady-like things.

'I can't fart on command, it only happens when I'm not expecting it. Sorry,' said Bogey, looking hopeless. He gave a little strain to see if anything was brewing.

'No... nothing.'

'I really cannot believe a lady could say such things,' announced Lord Itch, looking quite taken aback.

'You won't 'av to live with it for long, Itchy boy, here comes terra firma!' said Crane sarcastically.

'I know what'll get you going!' said Smell, jumping into action with a great idea.

'Turn around, Boges!'

'W-what… why, what you gonna do?' Bogey didn't like the sound of this. A great idea from Smell normally resulted in Bogey getting covered in something or at the very least coming out the very worst.

Bogey reluctantly turned around. And then…

BOOOOOOOOO!!!!! yelled Smell in Bogey's ear-hole.

The fright of Smell yelling as loud as you like caused the biggest farty explosion you have ever heard. The walls of the Love Bubble wobbled with the low frequency vibration as everyone hurried to mask their noses from the impending pong.

One by one, each of them broke out into a small giggle which grew into a louder chuckle until finally, by the time they had reached the ground, everyone was in a roar of side splitting hysterics. What a smelly scene…

The Love Bubble hovered for a moment above the Magic Carpet. It didn't know what to do, whether to shoot back up or to carry on trembling from all the vibrations…

Suddenly with an almighty *BANG!* the Love Bubble popped from the stress of it all, releasing the smelliest gust of air you have ever smelt: creatures who lived nearby quickly vacated the area; families packed up their belongings; ants broke out their gas masks and the authorities cordoned off the area within a ten-mile radius.

Everyone fell gently to the floor with a bump, landing on top of each other.

Chapter Seven

Dribble's Leap

'OH, clean air! Smell that fresh clean air!' said Fluff. Her hands were aloft praising the sky as she danced with joy.

'Ow, my back.'

'Oh, my head.'

'Ooh, me biscuits! I've landed on me biscuits!' Bogey looked positively peeved as crumbs fell from his pockets. He'd squashed his secret stash.

Everyone clambered to their feet, relieved that they'd survived the fall.

'It's Dribble's Leap! It's Dribble's Leap!' yelled Fluff, looking around to see the familiar sight of bare threaded carpet all around. Patches of carpet were frayed and worn so badly that you could see right through into the cellar below. A chilling wind howled through the gaps in the carpet and the treetops swayed with unease.

'Is everyone OK?' she said, checking everyone was accounted for.

'I'm OK but I've broken me biscuits!' Bogey harped on.

'Never mind your biscuits! Where's Smell?'

'Oh, I wondered what I was sitting on,' said Bogey as he picked himself up.

'Smell, are you alright?' Fluff asked, giving him a helping hand.

'GET OFF ME, YOU GOODY-GOODY TWO FACED FLIRT!' yelled Smell.

Fluff jumped back in shock; the others stood silently in bemusement.

'I say, old boy, that's no way to talk to a lady!' said Lord Itch, defending Fluff, who was close to bursting into tears.

'BACK OFF, YA LOW LIFE INSECT SCUM!! YOU PERTHETIC WASTE OF SPACE!!'

'Smelly, what's up, are you all right, you sound different... It's me... Boges... your old pal.'

'FRIEND... HA! YOU CALL YOURSELF A FRIEND... THAT'S A LAUGH! YOU DON'T KNOW THE MEANING OF THE WORD. I ONLY LIVE WITH YOU TO EAT THE FOOD YOU COOK... AND THAT'S ONLY SECOND RATE FLEA FODDER, FIT FOR THE LIKES OF GRUBS LIKE HIM!' Smell pointed to Crane as he dusted himself down.

Bogey backed off; something had clearly happened to Smell in the fall. The only time Smell had complained about his cooking was after the belly-bugs incident (but the recipe hadn't said you had to kill the bugs before putting them in the soup).

On hearing the 'flea fodder' comment, Crane stretched his legs to make himself look taller. They creaked and cracked as he towered into the air. He slowly moved toward Smell, who had changed appearance slightly. His face was bright red and his shape had been squashed. He was no longer slender and transparent, more squishy and yellowy in colour.

'Have ya got something to say to me, Smelly boy?' said Crane, who was surprisingly tall when he wanted to be.

'OH YEH… WE GONNA SEE SOME OF THAT OLD FLEA FIGHTING FORM YOU'VE BEEN BRAGGING ABOUT, HEY? DON'T MAKE ME LAUGH! YOU'RE FULL OF HOT AIR, CRANE. THE ONLY WAR YOU'VE EVER FOUGHT WAS THE INCH WAR!' Smell pointed at Crane's belly. Crane quickly breathed in to hide his bulge.

Immediately, Crane leapt onto Smell with such speed and started to scratch and bite. A flea's bite is deadly. Once blood is drawn, there's no stopping your blood from being sucked right out. Fleas had a deadly reputation in the Magic Carpet.

'Stop it, you two! Why are you fighting?' screamed Fluff, trying to get in the way of the brawl, but it was no use. Crane was letting Smell have it. His aggressive side was on show now; he tore and scratched chunks from Smell's arm as he pinned him down. His pointed teeth were protruding as he inched nearer to Smell's neck. Smell quickly whacked Crane between the legs. Crane let out an enormous yelp as he buckled over in pain. Smell jumped to his feet and ran to the edge of Dribble's Leap. He stopped just in time –

below where he stood was a great gaping hole in the carpet that plummeted into nothingness. The wind howled once again as he suddenly noticed something odd... Sticking out of the ground was a small stick, like a small flagpole, and attached to the top were a pair of old white underpants blowing in the wind. He quickly turned to face Crane, who had straightened back upright. He looked tall and menacing and very angry as he slowly crawled nearer and nearer, his one blood-red eye fixed intensely on Smell with hate and venom. Bogey, Fluff and the others watched on in horror as Crane towered over Smell at the edge of Dribble's Leap.

In a blink of an eye, Crane leapt into the air toward Smell. Smell quickly turned and reached for the flagpole, pulled it from the ground, removed the old underpants and impaled Crane in the shoulder as he landed on top.

AAAAHHHHH!!!!! screamed Crane in agony as he fell with a thud. The bare threads of carpet below twitched and jolted with the tension. And then...

TWANG!! The threads snapped with a violent jolt and Smell and Crane fell from Dribble's Leap and into the pit below.

'Smelly!' screamed Bogey as he clambered over the remaining threads of carpet to the torn edges. He peered down into blackness below trying to adjust his sight to see in the dark. Fluff followed, holding on to Bogey to steady him.

'Smelly!' he cried again in the hope he might've held on to the frayed edges as he fell in…

There was silence. No Smell. No Crane. Nothing.

Ding dong! went the front door of Mr and Mrs Mite, who lived not far from Dribble's Leap. They were just settling down for an evening cocoa and a game of Squabble, a popular game where you took turns to argue on a chosen subject.

'Who's that? At this time of night!' cried Mrs Mite half-way through her argument on the state of the Magic Carpet and whether the council should employ more weavers to repair the holes.

'Well, you're not gonna find out sitting there – off you go, gal!' replied Mr Mite as he lit up his pipe.

'Ya cheeky moo, there'll be no nibblin' in bed for you tonight if that's your attitude, me lad.'

Mr Mite pulled a funny face.

Ding dong!

'Ooh, I was just getting into that as well. Jot me points down so far, I won't be a widget.'

Mrs Mite got up from her comfy chair and went to answer the front door. Dust mites were funny creatures, tiny little bug-like things with massive eyes and always covered in dust. Every time they moved, dust would go everywhere. They loved to disagree and even if they thought you were right they'd argue you were wrong.

'Yes, 'ello, who's there?' said Mrs Mite, dusting herself down as she peered through the crack in the door.

There was absolute silence.

'Is it the gasman? 'Coz that boiler's playin' up again!' she shouted through the door. 'I haven't had a wink of sleep since you fiddled with it last time!'

'Why would the gasman be calling gone ten at night, ya dusty old mare?' said Mr Mite, coughing on his pipe.

'Hello! Is there anyone there?' she cried again. Losing interest, she turned away from the door toward her cocoa. And then…

KNOCK–KNOCK–KNOCK! boomed the door as the tiny little house shuddered. Dust drifted from the shelves, cupboards and windows.

Mrs Mite had had enough. She opened the front door to reveal an enormously tall figure dressed in a black cloak. He was so tall his head could not be seen. It reached far above the tiny doorway of the Mites' house.

'Ooh, I say… you're a tall one, aren't you. Who are you? What do you want at this time of night? Have you any idea what time it is?' Three questions in one sentence was quite restrained for Mrs Mite.

As before, the tall figure boomed out his warning.

'Uprising? Great danger? Leave right now, ya say? Ooh, I couldn't do that, me luv. I've just planted me hydrangeas – they won awards last year in the annual fair. I were reet pleased with the cuttings I got, wasn't I, dear?'

'Aye, that you were, me luv… Hey, do you remember what we did with ya winnings last year?' said Mr Mite in between several coughs caused by his smoky pipe. You could only just make out his silhouette from the murky haze that surrounded him.

'Ay, we went on that Eastern Bubble cruise, didn't we… What did that waiter call you on the second night, luv, d'ya remember?'

'The Mighty Love Machine!' said Mr Mite, proudly looking up from his pipe.

'The Mighty Love Machine – I ask you. You're about as romantic as a septic toe on a wet weekend to the Twisted Forest!'

The creature stood silent and confused in the doorway, wobbling slightly.

'BUT YOU ARE IN GREAT DANGER, YOU MUST ALL LEAVE NOW!!' he bellowed again. The cups of cocoa, which were rapidly going cold, tremoured on the coffee table. Dust filled the front room, cascading from the ceiling, rising from the carpet and falling from Mrs Mite's hair-do.

'OOH, ya silly moo!' Mrs Mite shouted as she dusted herself down once again.

Just then a familiar noise could be heard beneath their feet.

THUD THUMP – THUD THUMP – THUD THUMP – THUD THUMP!!! This time the noise was very intense and felt very close. The Mites' whole house shuddered wildly as dust plumes filled the room. Mrs Mite screamed in panic as she quickly reached for her duster. Poor old Mr Mite had disappeared in a cloud of dust and smoke. All you could see were a pair of slippers. All you could hear were his coughs and splutters. There was dust everywhere.

Back at Dribble's Leap, Fluff comforted Bogey as he dangled his legs over the edge of the pit. He looked very glum and wasn't saying much.

'I'm sure he didn't suffer, old bean,' said Lord Itch, trying to think of something helpful to say.

Just then the whole carpet around them shuddered.

THUD THUMP – THUD THUMP – THUD THUMP – THUD THUMP!!!

Bogey quickly grabbed onto Fluff as she pulled him away from the edge. The remaining friends clambered to a safe distance from the edge while the noise continued. Bits and pieces were falling from the thread tops as Bogey, Fluff, Crumb and Lord Itch huddled together for safety. As night fell in the Magic Carpet the remaining crew of Operation Ginger Storm were now down to four…

'Well, if my calculations are correct, the uprising is imminent,' said Lord Itch as he stood guard over the camp. The ground still trembled with the thumping noise; the constant drumming was all around them.

'I know a really good song that'll cheer us up,' said Crumb as he prodded the campfire. Nobody responded.

'What do you think the uprising is?' Fluff asked Lord Itch. Bogey was sleeping next to her and for the first time ever he wasn't snoring.

'Well, whatever it is, I think we're out-numbered,' Lord Itch said, scratching his head.

'I say we fight! We can't give in and let whoever it is invade our home,' Crumb announced in a moment of hollow passion. 'Of course, I have no idea how we fight… with no weapons, no army and no experience.'

The fire crackled and spluttered as the night air became sharper around them.

'I say, wait one moment, old bean! We do have an army, you know. My chaps back at H.Q.!' Lord Itch stood to attention inspired by his great idea. The antennas on his head stood up tall like excited hairs and wiggled with hope.

'My chaps can fight – they're trained to the highest standard you know. Queen and Country and all that!'

That night, as dusk fell upon the Magic Carpet, Lord Itch set out his plan of action. He would go back and fetch his ant army while the others would continue forward to Ginger Bags the cat. If all else failed, then Ginger Bags would surely know what to do.

The carpet became very cold at Dribble's Leap that night. Drafts would get in the most unusual of places. Bogey, Fluff and Crumb were fast asleep by the campfire while Lord Itch packed his backpack and kept watch like a true soldier. The ground was still shaking and the noises were all around. Suddenly something appeared in the forest that stopped Lord Itch's heart dead.

'I say,' he thought. His feet were frozen to the spot. He slowly knelt down to appear less noticeable.

'This must be it,' he muttered aloud, quickly arming himself with a feeble hot stick he found in the fire.

'Err, I say, chaps, you might want to wake up for this!' Lord Itch was backing away from two hideous blood-red eyes fixed on him in an evil stare. He couldn't make out any shape to the creepy creature, just two hungry eyes watching from the forest. Then another pair of eyes appeared to the right, then another pair appeared to the left and yet another. Lord Itch was totally surrounded. The thud–thumping noises were coming from the feet of these creatures as they marched. The carpet tops shuddered with apprehension, the creatures hissed and clicked as they crawled closer and closer. The Magic Carpet buzzed with the throng of impending doom.

'Err, I really do think you ought to wake up this very minute!' he cried again, this time a decibel louder, but still no movement.

'WAKE UP… AAAHHHH!!!'

The others woke up with a jolt to see Lord Itch running off into the carpet being chased by thousands of silhouetted creatures with piercing red eyes, clicking and creaking as they scurried after him.

Bogey, Fluff and Crumb screamed as they jumped to their feet to see hundreds of thousands of blood-thirsty *fleas* heading right for them, fangs out and ready to carve up anything that stood in their way.

THUD–THUMP–THUD–THUMP! The swarm marched out from Dribble's Leap and infested the Magic Carpet.

Chapter Eight

The Pit

'Ow, my head.'

The intense darkness imposed itself into every nook and cranny, overwhelming the mind and numbing the senses. A bitter howling wind blew past his ears as his eyesight adjusted to this hostile place. Flecks of white light managed to reach shiny surfaces on the floor around him, rcflccting on strange looking shapes on the ground. A sharp pain, rushing down his legs and into his toes, awoke his dazed senses as he bolted upright.

'Ow!'

He sensed something close in the darkness, as if he were being watched, so he turned to his left…

'AAAAHHHHH!!!!' Two blood-red eyes were staring right at him inches away. He jumped to his feet in an instant and leapt into the air. In a frenzied panic, he ran as fast as he could, only to fall after a few yards onto something soft. The ground felt strange and uneven. He paused to catch his breath, his heart rate going double time.

'Where am I?' he thought, trying to focus on something familiar in the darkness.

Just then a creaking noise came from behind him. He jumped and froze stiff in fright as a sense of dread and fear fizzed through his veins.

He looked up to the distant glow that shone from above. Columns of light shone down like rainfall.

'Bogey... Fluff...!' he thought to himself as the realisation of who and what he was crept back into his mind.

'What happened to me?' Smell thought, remembering his behaviour at Dribble's Leap.

'It must've been Bogey's intoxicating pong,' he thought, scratching his head. Smell was, after all, a *smell* and being around other strong whiffs often had strange effects on him. Just then something began to move by his feet. The darkness did not let up; he inched backward silently as the rustling turned into...

'Blimey... What hit me? Man, that was heavy.'

Smell stood silently over the voice, trying not to breath or blink or he'd be spotted.

''Ello! Who's that?' the voice demanded. The small figure got to his feet and stood trying to focus on what was in front of him.

''Ello, I know ya there, I can make you out.' The figure moved closer and then...

'Ow!!!' The creature fell stumbling to the floor.

'Ooh, are you all right?' said Smell.

'Ah ha! You are there!' said the voice.

'Who is it? I recognise the voice… It's all right, you can trust me.'

There was a brief pause. And then…

'I'm Smell… who are you?'

It went silent again…

'Smell?' the voice cried out in surprise.

'Smell? As in Smell and Bogey and Fluff?'

'Yes – why, have you heard of me?' said Smell, intrigued.

'Heard of you? You're my only hope, boy!' The voice got nearer and more excited.

Just then creaking and clicking could be heard from all around them. The ground began to move and wriggle.

'Quick, Smell, we better get out of here, it's not safe y'know.'

From the darkness appeared more blood-red eyes. They were everywhere and closing in fast. The two lonely figures trapped in the pit ran into the depths of the void, dodging the red-eyed creatures that ran at them from every direction. The friendly figure held on to Smell's hand tight. His voice seemed familiar but Smell couldn't place it.

'What's your name, by the way?' Smell asked as they ran blindly in the darkness.

'Ow!!' screamed the figure as he fell onto something very big and squidgey. Smell soon followed the downward direction, ending up in what felt like the arms of something very, very large and gooey.

'Ooh, whart have we here then?' rumbled a large female voice in a slightly Scottish accent. Smell and his new friend stared up at the impossible view before their eyes. A thousand beaming eyeballs of every shape, size and colour were fixed intensely on the pair; two giant tentacle-like arms had grabbed hold of them. Smell's eyesight was beginning to get used to his new surroundings. He could only just make out what had got hold of them; he couldn't explain it, but he sure could see it. 'It' being the operative word.

Stretched out before them was a giant slimy blob with eyes and tentacles – the most ugly sight you have ever seen. Air pockets appeared in random places on its skin, releasing hideous wafts of pongy wind. The noise and the smell were intense.

'Eyerene!' shouted Smell's new friend. Twelve or so of the eyes quickly turned to focus on the voice. Suddenly her grasp loosened slightly.

'Aye, it's Dribble! Girls, look, it's our Dribble!' All the eyes turned toward him, chuckling and cooing as a thousand eyelids blinked and winked in his general direction. Farty squelches and pops let off gasses of excitement.

'How are ye going, me lad? And who, may I ask, is this fine specimen of a man, ay?' The tentacle holding Smell tightened as it lifted him closer to one of the bigger eyes.

'Oh, that's Smell of Smell and Bogey!' cried Dribble. Smell looked at Dribble in shock and amazement. He was not how he'd imagined him at all. He'd always thought of Dribble as a powerful figure, dashing and brave, your typical superhero type. Instead, standing before him was a ghostly pale shell of a figure, aged and tired with saddened eyes, slightly transparent like Smell, a splodgy shape with a deep scar running down his right cheek.

'I thought you were dead! You disappeared years ago!'

'Disappeared, yeah, but not dead. Well, not quite,' said Dribble.

'And whart brings yee to these neck of the glooms?' asked Eyerene, positively inspired to have company. You can imagine the noise and odour by now.

'Have you not heard of the uprising?' asked Smell, trying to dodge the smelly wafts coming his way.

'Uprising? Whart uprising?'

'The fleas are invading the Magic Carpet!' said Dribble.

'Fleas y'say!' Some of her eyes looked at each other with interest, a few of them raised the odd eyebrow.

'Well, good riddance I say.'

Smell, Dribble and Eyerene talked for a while. Smell hadn't realised it was *fleas* trying to invade the Magic Carpet. His home would never be the same again if they infested it, he thought, while looking at Eyerene, trying to work out what sort of creature she was.

'Does it ever get any brighter down here? asked Smell, now back on terra firma.

'Afraid not, boy,' said Dribble.

'And whatever ya do, don't let go of those underpants you're still holding!'

Smell looked down at his hand to see he was still clutching onto the grotty old pair of pants he'd picked up at Dibble's Leap.

'Why, what's so special about these?'

'Have ye never heard of Hover-Pants before, me laddie?' exclaimed Eyerene.

'Hover-Pants?' questioned Smell, looking puzzled.

'Yeah, that's your only means of escape from the pit. You best try 'em on and get some practice in,' said Dribble.

Smell tried on the pants and stood in the twilight looking like a right lemon. Dribble and Eyerene couldn't contain themselves any more. They both burst out into the noisiest roar of laughter. Squelchy puffs of pongy splutter came shooting out of Eyerene's air holes.

'SSSSHHHHHHHH!' cried Dribble, suddenly realising the fleas could be anywhere.

'So what happens now, then?' whispered Smell, not feeling very comfortable in someone else's grotty old pants.

'Hold ya breath!' cried Dribble, sitting down to get comfy.

Smell frowned at Dribble. Every eye of Eyerene's was now focused rigidly on Smell and his new underpants. Smell paused for a minute, not believing a word of this far-fetched notion…

'Hover-Pants indeed,' he thought. He took a few deep breaths and then stopped. Suddenly he shot up vertically out of sight and into the gloomy darkness above with such speed he could hardly catch his breath.

'AAAARRRRGGGGHHHH!!!!' he yelled as he came hurtling back down.

'There he goes!' cried Dribble, pointing at the strangest looking superhero with white underpants, flying through the columns of light that shone from above. He chuckled to himself at the thought of what Smell's superhero name would be. 'Captain Underpants!' he thought.

'Wow! They really do work!' said Smell as he plonked back down to earth.

'Yeah, but you're gonna have to practise take-off and landing if you're to get out of here. Hover-Pants are quite hard to master; you can end up anywhere if ya not careful,' said Dribble.

Smell continued to practise take-off and landing, holding small breaths for slow take-offs and big breaths for giant leaps...

'Wow! This is so much fun!' cried Smell as he dusted down his new pair of pants, forgetting for a moment his lost friends and the impending doom above.

'Have you got a pair, Dribble?'

'Me... Ah, no boy, I don't need Hover-Pants...' he said sadly.

Eyerene quickly butted in and started to explain how Hover-Pants worked, the clever tricks you could do in mid flight and how they were great for getting out of tricky situations.

'OK, OK, I think I've understood all that,' said Smell, feeling like he'd just had intense military training on the art of flying your pants.

'So let's try something big!' said Smell, feeling confident.

'If I'm going to escape from the pit, I'm going to need to hold my breath for a long time. It looks awfully high up there.' Smell pointed to the tatty frayed edges of the Magic Carpet. It seemed like miles and miles away and the thought of ever getting back was beginning to seem impossible.

'All right, boy, now remember everything we've taught you and watch that landing too. Blow out slowly as you come back down.'

Dribble checked the elastic on Smell's pants and pulled them up tightly ready for the ride of his life.

'See if ye can reach the underneath of the Magic Carpet,' said Eyerene, all eyes looking skyward.

'OK, here we go then – stand back, this is going to be a big one!' said Smell, looking surprisingly confident.

Smell looked at one of Eyerene's largest eyes then turned to look at Dribble. Dribble gave him the thumbs up to signify all being ready for launch.

'3… 2… 1…' Smell took the deepest breath ever and in a blink of an eye disappeared vertically in a *Whoosh*!

Silence crept into the pit. Eyerene and Dribble looked at each other then up at the Magic Carpet. Nothing. Nothing at all. No movement. No noise. Nothing. Smell had completely and utterly vanished from…

Suddenly, with an almighty sneeze and a gust of snotty wind…

'AAAARRRRGGGGHHHH-TISSSSUUUUEEEE!!!!'

PING!

Smell and his grotty white pants went flying through the air, but instead of going up he was travelling horizontally from left to right.

'Smell!!' cried Dribble. Eyerene's beady eyes were all closed, braced ready for the inevitable crash landing.

'AAAARRRRGGGGHHHH!!!!' screamed Smell.

'Follow that scream!' yelled Dribble, desperately trying to follow Captain Underpants as he whizzed through the air at the speed of sneeze. Pretty fast.

Smell came to a rather sticky but thankfully bouncy full stop as he crashed into what felt like a sticky trampoline. But once his eyes had acclimatised again he realised what he'd landed on.

'Spider-web!' he thought out loud, tugging and wriggling to try to free himself.

'DRIBBLE!' he yelled, looking for his new friend in the pit of darkness.

'MELLLY!' came a muffled distant response.

Smell had been trapped in spider-web before and it wasn't good. The shock waves from the web sent a signal to whoever had spun it... It was like ringing the *dinner bell.*

'Will you stop wriggling, I'm tryin' ta get sum rest!' came a wheezy old voice from the shadows.

'Who's that?' jumped Smell, looking to his left, catching a glimpse of something rather dangly and very close.

''Ere, don't listen to him, me boy, he's a right grumpy old dirt bag!' came another wheezy voice, this time on Smell's right. Smell quickly turned his head and squinted.

'I ain't no dirt bag, ya dribbling little bum bag!'

'I ain't no bum bag, ya brain the size of a grain of sand that's been diced into quarters and sold off for dung beetle food!'

'Ah, at least I have a brain, Mr Thick Thickerdy Thickerson, the son of Mrs No-Brains!'

'Dust mites!' thought Smell.

Several hours later, after the conversion had dredged the very lowest realms of the English language, Smell had grown a rather jaunty beard and decided to take up watching paint dry for a living after this particular adventure had concluded. Suddenly…

EEEEEEECK!!! CLICK, CLICK, CLICK!

The stale, still air around them started to blow and howl. A warm and unfriendly smell carried on the breeze. A very uneasy thought popped into Smell's head… Whoever had made that noise didn't sound like the sort chap you wanted to sit down and have tea with.

'GROWL!' went his empty belly, at the thought of tea.

'Will you two be quiet! Didn't you hear that?' shouted Smell in a whisper. The two dust mites looked up from their row and froze stiff, eyes twitching and hearts pounding…

EEEEEEECK!!! CLICK, CLICK, CLICK!

Smell and the dust mites wriggled frantically to get free from their sticky trap. Dust clouded Smell's view as he tugged in panic, only to get tangled up even more. He tried to focus on anything out in the murky darkness ahead. The clicking and screaming got louder and more ear piercing. Suddenly a flash of movement and then the unmistakable shape of long dark hairy legs. It could only mean one thing…

EEEEEEECK!!!!!

There he stood in all his glory, *if you like spiders, that is*. A giant, hideous, eight legged, dribbling, hairy monster, fangs gleaming, eight eyes twitching and legs clicking and stomping in excitement.

'Three courses for dinner!' thought Fangs as he danced and paraded up and down in anticipation.

'Oh, I'm gonna enjoy this so much,' he thought. Spiders often had to go for long periods of time without food and this particularly day had been very lean. Fangs sharpened his gnashers as Smell and the others turned their heads away trembling, braced for the end. Eight hideous bulging eyes twitched and then with his mouth wide open…

''Ello Fangs!' came a friendly cry from the darkness below.

Fangs' gob quickly shut tight in shock as he looked down and squinted at the ground.

'Over 'ere, me old mate!' came the voice again.

Fangs looked around puzzled and irritated – was he ever going to get any dinner today?

'Oh, hello Dribble, click click!' bellowed Fangs, spotting the faded figure standing at his feet.

'How ya getting on?' asked Dribble, as he leant on one of Fangs' legs.

'Oh, *click*, can't complain. Well, I could, *click*, but it wouldn't do any good, *click*. Me gammy leg's playing up again. You know I can hardly walk in the morning these days. Rigid I am, rigid, *click*!'

'Didn't seem very rigid to me this morning,' mumbled Smell, relieved to see Dribble. In an instant Fangs bolted his attention back at Smell, slime pouring from his chops and all eyes twitching.

'Excuse me, click, for a moment Dribble, but I must have something to eat. I'm, *click*, starving y'know!'

'Wait!!' yelled Dribble as Fangs opened his mouth wide.

'You can't eat him!'

'Eh, click, and why not?'

'*He* is Smell and *he* is going to help us get rid of the fleas once and for all!' cried Dribble, hoping his plea would cut it with a very hungry and powerful spider.

'Is he really, *click, click*! Well, you're braver than you look, boy!' exclaimed Fangs, slightly uninterested. By now he'd given up on ever eating today; every time he got even close to lunch something got in his way or his lunch would run away.

'I really should become a vegetarian,' thought a very disgruntled spider.

Smell, Dribble, Fangs and the dust mites sat together and talked in the gloom about the uprising and what could be done. Smell couldn't believe the day he was having. Here he was having a polite conversation with a giant spider, he'd discovered that Dribble was alive and he'd learnt how to fly, somewhat badly.

That evening, Dribble went into great detail about his plan to warn the others in the Magic Carpet with the help of Smell's Hover-Pants. And with Fangs now on board and the ant army led by Lord Itch, things looked a lot less desperate. By morning, 'Operation De-bug' would fling into action.

Nights in the pit were not just dark but very dark, very cold and very dangerous. All sorts of grotesque, deranged creatures crawled in this hellish place at night. Smell, Dribble and the mites huddled together under the protection of Fangs, who had rolled up his eight spindly legs into a hairy barricade. Droplets of water could be heard echoing in all directions followed by the odd crazy scream from some mad creature trapped in the shadows.

From the darkness flecks of light flashed from shiny dark creatures crawling the walls of the basement, all heading in one direction… UP! Then came the all too familiar sound that had haunted our friends from the very start… the sound of the Uprising. The flea army was invading!

THUD – THUMP! THUD – THUMP! THUD – THUMP! THUD – THUMP!

Chapter Nine

The Uprising!

'I can't keep running! I'm bored of running. All I want is to get on with that pile of ironing back at home!' moaned Bogey, his big belly bouncing up and down as he ran through the Magic Carpet, chased by swarms and swarms of crazy, hungry fleas.

'There won't be any ironing, home or anything left if this lot get their way!' said Fluff, clutching her waist in pain.

'What are we gonna do?' cried little Crumb. His legs were a lot smaller and he was running out of steam fast.

'*Jammy sandwich, blueberry muffin, apple pie, treacle sponge... Bread and butter pudding, spotted dick and custard, Yum yummy, for my tea.*' Bogey sang his favourite food song as he waddled from side to side, drunk on exhaustion.

'What in the Magic Carpet was that?' asked Fluff.

'It's my favourite food song. I sing it when I'm stressed or nervous,' said Bogey. 'It works wonders. As soon as I think of food, I don't feel stressed any more. We should all sing it, it'll help!' exclaimed Bogey, positively excited.

So Bogey, Crumb and a reluctant Fluff sang as they ran for their lives through the Magic Carpet…

'Jammy sandwich, blueberry muffin, apple pie, treacle sponge… Bread and butter pudding, spotted dick and custard, Yum yummy, for my tea.'

'And again, everybody after three… one, two, thr...!'

'Wait, Bogey, quiet and get down!' yelled Fluff, who was way out in front of the boys and had spotted something up ahead.

Bogey's cheery disposition soon disappeared as the image of piping hot treacle sponge smothered in thick delicious custard faded from his thoughts.

Out in front of them stood a small and dusty old house with a tiny little door half open. All around dust hovered in the air, strangely calm and peaceful, the threads of Magic Carpet that surrounded the house were twisted and matted together.

'What is it, Fluff?' Crumb called from his hiding position.

Bogey too had opted for a hiding position, but Fluff was walking straight up to the little house, bravely tip toeing as she went.

'I think someone's in,' she whispered, 'they're in great danger.'

'So are you, ya daft fluffball!' said Bogey, trying to cover himself with strands of carpet for camouflage.

Fluff gently pushed the little door open, concerned for the occupants. Dust flew everywhere as she walked in through the haze.

'Fluff! Will you come out, they might be getting ready for bed or doing stuff or something!' cried Bogey quietly. He looked at Crumb, who had also fashioned hairy camouflage from scraps of carpet.

'Come on, Crumb, we're going in!' said Lieutenant Bogey reluctantly…

'Fluff, where are you?' whispered Bogey as he crept through the dusty room followed by Crumb. The pair looked liked hairy soldiers, stealthily surveying every inch of the room as they entered. The room had been ransacked, family pictures lay on the floor, crockery had been smashed, someone's knitting was strewn on the family rug and by the leg of a comfy chair lay a smouldering pipe.

'Fluff, are you in here?' whispered Bogey.

'Over here, Boges,' came a familiar voice.

Bogey and Crumb crept toward the voice through the impossibly thick dust that was tickling Bogey's already dry throat.

Gurgle! went his empty belly.

As the dust thinned he could just make out Fluff peering over someone sitting in another comfy chair. He moved closer, followed by Crumb. They both peered over Fluff's shoulder and…

'AAARRRGGGHHH!!!!!'   screamed Bogey and Crumb together.

Dust flew up everywhere as the two boys ran as quickly as they could to get away from the hideous sight. Sitting in the chair was the hollowed out remains of Mrs Mite, her face was transparent and distorted with pain. All the blood in her body had been sucked out; just a shell remained. Bent over her lap, was Mr Mite, also sucked dry of every ounce of life. A few tears welled up in Fluff's eyes as she turned to leave.

'Wait, come back!' she yelled as she ran out of the house after Bogey and Crumb. Suddenly from every direction came the sound…

THUD – THUMP, THUD – THUMP, CREAK, CRACKLE AND SCREAM!

The flea army swarmed in from every direction – a flowing tide of crawling, hungry, red-eyed creatures. They jumped onto anything that moved and tore shreds off their prey. They gnawed at the twisted carpet and devoured everything in sight. Nothing stood a chance.

Bogey and Crumb stood frozen to the spot in the middle of all the commotion but the fleas seemed to ignore them…

'Stand very still and don't move a muscle!' yelled Fluff, who was still in the doorway of the Mites' house. Suddenly all the fleas turned toward the voice, their blood-red eyes hungry for more. They pounced onto her, engulfing the little fluff ball, her snowy white body turning into a mound of black as she fell to the floor.

'CHAAAAAAARGE!!!' came the voices of two of the silliest soldiers you have ever seen. Bogey and Crumb ran toward the mountain of fleas wearing their hairy camouflage, Bogey's belly bouncing and Crumb's little legs going double time. Just then another call to 'Charge' was heard from the forest, this time from a well-spoken and more authoritarian voice.

'Left right, left right, left right, left right!' came the cries from Lord Itch and his ant army, marching with such pride and dignity. His head was held high in the air. Over his shoulders was draped a red and gold embroidered cloak.

'Company... halt!' he cried with such charm, flicking the dust from his cloak with his velvet handkerchief. Behind him, hundreds of ants came to a sudden standstill with precision, each brandishing their own choice of weapon. Shoulders back, chests out and standing ready to spring into action for queen and country. Behind them, coming to a wobbly halt, the strangest sight you have ever seen. Ten or more of the smallest ants stood bent over in agony, dripping with sweat, knees trembling with the stress of carrying the hugest, fattest creature ever. The Queen of the Ants lay, not exactly regally, a huge overweight blubbery whale of a thing, rolling from side to side, one cotton gloved hand waving to the crowds while the other stuffed her face with all sorts of food. In went a grape and a creamy cake, a headless bug and a slimy slug.

'Ooh, I say… Has one arrived?' exclaimed the Queen with a mouthful, looking down at the dusty commotion taking place below.

'Err, yes, Ma'am, our journey is at its end. Would you like to dismount?' Lord Itch bowed with such grace.

'Umm, no! I'll stay up here and watch, thank you,' declared her royal blubbery-ness. The poor squashed ants below let out a restrained but polite cry as one of them buckled with the pressure.

'Splat!' went the poor little chap.

'Lord Itch, try and keep these fellows focused on their jobs!' cried the Queen, who had almost missed her mouth completely with a particularly creamy cake.

'Err, yes, Ma'am! Err, permission to get... stuck in?' Lord Itch bowed before his Queen, draping his scarlet cloak around his shoulders.

'Stuck in? Oh yes, quite... Go and get them, Tiger!' cried the Queen.

Just then Lord Itch and a hundred of his finest men leapt into battle, jumping onto the fleas' backs to avoid their deadly fangs. Dust and debris flew everywhere as twenty or more ants charged towards the giant mound of fleas that were trying to devour Bogey and Crumb.

'Help, help!' screamed Bogey, who wasn't really cut out to be a fighter. There was no sign of Fluff as the ants piled on top of the already huge mound of creatures.

'Fluff... Fluff! Are you here?' cried Bogey as one flea started nibbling on his foot.

'Ah! Get off you pesky thing!' he screamed as he flicked his leg, sending the hideous creature flying into the air. He landed right on top of the Queen's cream cake, but the Queen had already opened her royal trap and…

'GOBBLE!' the Queen munched her way through a rather crispy and bitter chocolate sponge pudding.

'Crunchy?' she thought to herself.

The fight was ferocious. There were ants' and fleas' bodies all over the place. The dust went up into the air and plumes could be seen for miles around. Lord Itch had got his men to fall back to the forest. They were totally out-numbered and more fleas were swarming in from every direction. They were relentless. Screams and cries could be heard coming from all over the Magic Carpet. Just then, from under the enormous mound of creatures came a familiar voice.

'Quiet and listen!' yelled Crumb.

'What is it? Bogey replied.

'I can here Fluff, I'm sure of it!' Crumb was bending over, trying to stay on top of the mound and keep his balance.

'What's she saying?' asked Bogey. He'd now got two fleas nibbling on both feet.

'AAH, AAH, AAH! I think...?' said Crumb. His ears twitched and wriggled.

'AAH, AAH, AAH?' questioned Bogey.

'I'm sure of it… Wait! There it goes again!'

Sure enough, under all the commotion and noise, you could just about make out Fluff's voice…

'AAH, AAH, AAH… TISSUUUUUE!!!'

Well, for such a polite and refined fluff ball, the noise and gusty snottyness that blew from her sweet hooter was immense. Bogey and Crumb flew high into the air, both landing on the tops of the twisted carpet threads. Fleas' bodies went whizzing in every direction, screaming, with legs kicking as they flew….

As the dust settled in the Magic Carpet, sitting upright in the middle of what was a huge mound of creatures now sat a single white ball of fluff.

'Fluff!' yelled Crumb, looking down from the treetops as he swayed.

'Hide quickly, Fluff!' yelled Bogey. He could see more fleas coming their way and they looked very hungry. Fluff quickly jumped to her feet and turned to run into the forest, but as soon as she entered, standing before her stood a deformed and broken figure with one blood-red eye staring at her with hatred and venom. The figure creaked and snapped as it slowly moved toward her. Fluff started to back off slowly into open ground. It was getting lighter in the Magic Carpet. The greys and blacks of the night were now violets and rich blues. As Fluff stood frozen to the spot, Bogey looked down from the carpet tops to see *Crane* hunched over his little fluffy friend and behind him a thousand or more fleas, clambering impatiently to get their fix.

'Crane!' exclaimed Fluff, backing slowly.

'What are you doing? I thought you didn't fight any more?'

'It's in me blood, see! I've tasted too many to give up now and there's one more I want to taste before I truly retire!' Crane snarled, flashing his fangs. They shone in the morning light, his one blood-red eye squinting and twitching as he pushed little Fluff up against the carpet thread that Bogey and Crumb still clung to.

'Excuse me, if you don't mind, I think you'll find this dance is mine!' Crane backed off instantly at the sight of Lord Itch, peering down on him from out of the darkness. His cloak was in tatters and he'd been bitten all over, but he wasn't going to let that stop him giving this old has-been a damn good thrashing.

Crane straightened up to equal Lord Itch's height and leapt instantly, tearing and scratching at the ant's body like a wild animal. From behind both leaders surged their armies, the fleas outnumbering the ants. It didn't look good so Fluff, Bogey and Crumb quietly snuck away into the hazy dawn, walking even deeper into the Magic Carpet.

Fluff, Bogey and Crumb had only gone a few paces when suddenly, in the blink of an eye, the tall hooded figure with the horrible red eyes appeared in front of them, blocking their path.

'STOP! YOU ARE IN GREAT DANGER!' boomed the sinister voice. The figure wobbled slightly.

After all they'd been through, bumping into this lanky door-to-door salesman was the last of their worries.

'Err… thank you, Einstein. I don't know where we'd be without your profound wisdom!' shouted Bogey confidently from behind Fluff's shoulder.

'We know we are in great danger, can you help by any chance?' said Fluff politely.

'FOLLOW US TO THE TWISTED FOREST. THERE YOU WILL FIND YOUR JOURNEY'S END!'

'Follow us?' said Fluff.

'Journey's end?' said Crumb.

'I wish I'd stayed at home!' said Bogey.

The figure did not talk or respond to their many questions as they walked at dawn. Everywhere they looked there were shells of bodies, all drained of blood; they looked like crystal sculptures gleaming in the morning light. Then after about thirty minutes or so…

'WE REST HERE AND WAIT!' boomed the hooded figure as he stopped and turned, pointing at an open bit of ground. The Magic Carpet threads were very twisted and frayed.

'This must be the Twisted Forest.' said Crumb, looking up at the curly treetops. Bogey was the first to take up the opportunity to put his feet up. He plonked himself down and thought of his favourite thing… cake. Dribble gathered at one corner of his mouth and slowly oozed to the floor.

Just then, before his disbelieving eyes… the juiciest, richest, treacle sponge topped with lashings of rich double cream appeared by his feet, smiling at him. Bogey was mesmerised for a moment. Then in an instant, he slammed his entire face into the sweetest of cakes, with not one thought of the mess it would cause.

'I have died and gone to heaven, that's the only explanation for it!' he thought, but he wasn't about to argue one bit.

Crumb rubbed his head, looking puzzled.

'How did you do that, Bogey?' he asked, getting hunger pains.

'I just thought of cake and there it was!' cried Bogey, with the biggest smile on his face.

Crumb stood for a moment in deep thought. He closed his eyes, then his ears pricked upright with an idea. Immediately before him appeared a bathtub full to the brim of the thickest, creamiest, darkest runny chocolate. Crumb wasted no time and with toes on the rim, took one giant leap and dived into chocolate heaven.

SPLOOOOOSH! Chocolate droplets went everywhere. Bogey quickly sprang into action, licking up the excess chocolate on all fours.

The tall hooded figure stood menacingly quiet and turned to Fluff.

'Oh, me?' exclaimed Fluff.

'I don't need cakes and chocolate, thanks.'

'You don't know what you're missing, Fluffy!' yelled Bogey who had now joined Crumb in his bathtub of chocolate. They were splashing and rolling around like children at bath-time.

The hooded figure pointed to her with a long spindly finger. Fluff sat down and thought for a moment.

It suddenly got cold and dark in the Twisted Forest, then a glowing white light shone from deep within the woodland. It started to move; it was getting nearer and nearer. Bogey stopped munching for a minute and looked up from his bath, runny chocolate dribbling from his happy chops.

Fluff stared intensely with pretty, wide-open eyes as the glowing cloud of light entered the opening. It throbbed and hummed with energy and power.

'Hello!' she cried, looking into the light standing before her.

'Fluff! Is that you?' a distant voice replied.

Fluff put her hands to her mouth and tears began to fill up her dreamy brown eyes.

'Fluff! Where are ya? I can't see ya, but it is you, isn't it?'

'Yes, it's me!' replied Fluff, bursting into tears.

'Don't cry, sweetie, I'm fine, and don't worry, I'm with you always. Just dream and I'm there.'

Fluff fell to her knees sobbing and distraught, a hundred emotions whizzing through her head, her heart pounding heavily as Bogey and Crumb dashed to comfort her, covering Fluff in chocolate and treacle.

Nobody said much that morning. The hooded figure just stood, wobbling occasionally. Bogey and Crumb helped clean Fluff down once she'd stopped sobbing. And despite wanting to, nobody asked whom the voice belonged to. But they could guess.

'I wonder which way to Ginger Bags from here?' pondered Crumb, looking around at the Twisted Forest. It looked thick and foreboding.

Suddenly, rumbles and shakes came from all around, cracks and snaps echoed in the morning light and then before their eyes the Twisted Forest threads parted a way, revealing a single track before them. Dust and debris fell from the treetops as light shone in, carving a route deeper into the Magic Carpet.

Chapter Ten

Ginger Bags

'Well, there's your answer,' said Fluff.

'Can we trust it?' said Bogey, looking concerned, not relishing the idea of even more walking.

'GO!' said the tall hooded figure, pointing at the opening in the forest. So Fluff, Bogey and Crumb led the way followed menacingly by the hooded figure through the Twisted Forest. Deeper and deeper into the Magic Carpet they went. Every ten minutes or so the carpet would rustle and sway, opening up another route before them. It was very un-nerving. Every noise and gusty howl made Bogey and Crumb flinch in fright.

'I think my feet are gonna drop off any second,' moaned Bogey. By now he was having hallucinations of every type of cake imaginable in the hope that another one would suddenly become reality.

'I've gotta rest too, Boges,' said Fluff.

'I think we need some proper rest. I can't remember the last time we had a good sleep.' Fluff sat down against a fluffy orange part of the carpet and yawned. Crumb sat beside her and leant on the fluffy surface. It was very soft and very soothing.

'Well, I'm gonna have a look up here before I fall asleep – you never know how close those pesky fleas are!' Bogey was trying to climb up the orange embankment that led to a good vantage point above.

'Oh, wow, you can see for miles and miles up here!' he said, reaching the top of the hill.

'Any sign of the fleas?' shouted Crumb. Poor old Fluff was out like a light.

'No, it's all clear from here!'

'It's really soft and comfy, isn't it? I might settle down for a few winks myself.' Bogey rested his feet and leant back on the fluffy, orange hill.

The tall hooded figure just stood tall and hooded, still wobbling occasionally; he too was looking a little weary. Bogey looked down at him and wondered what he was and why he was helping. What did he look like under the hood, if indeed he was a he? It could be a she or a hideously deformed monster with no eyes and giant fangs ready to devour them all as soon as they nodded off to sleep. Bogey shivered with the thought as he rested his head. He decided to keep lookout whilst his two remaining friends slept below. Thoughts of Smell crept into his head and the memories of the wonderful times they'd had together trickled into his mind. Even though living with Smell hadn't always been easy, or tidy for that matter, now Smell was gone, Bogey realised he felt lonely and sad…

YAAAAAAWNNN!

Bogey sat upright. Dazed, he looked down at his two friends below. They were still fast asleep, but the hooded figure was staring intently up at him with his blood-red eyes fixed fast.

YAAAAAAWNNN! went the sound again.

'Who in the Magic Carpet is that?' Bogey thought, looking around confused.

'Hey, you two, wake up down there!' he cried.

'VOICES IN ME 'ED NOW, VOICES IN ME 'ED! ME LUGS ARE PLAYING TRICKS, OR IT'S TRUE WHAT THEY SAY, I'M AS NUTTY AS THOSE BADGERS!'

By now Fluff and Crumb were wide-awake and as confused as Bogey.

'KIPPERS WOULD BE NICE, I HAVEN'T HAD A GOOD NIBBLE IN… OOH, IT'S BIN LONGER THAN THAT I SHOULD THINK.'

Bogey jumped from the fluffy mound and landed on Crumb's big toe.

'OW!'

They all looked up to where the sound seemed to be coming from. But all they could see was a giant orange mound of fluff before them. Suddenly two black round objects appeared side by side in amongst the fluff. They shone and glistened as light reflected off them. Something in the middle twitched and wriggled. A strong gust of wind blew past Bogey's ears. And then…

AAAAGGGGHHHH-
TISSSSUUUUEEEE!!!!

Bogey, Fluff, Crumb and the hooded figure flew on the cold, snotty breeze that whooshed from a giant pair of nostrils. They ended up flung against the carpet wall opposite, covered in mucus and fishy bits. Crumb ricocheted off Bogey's big bulging belly and bounced vertically into the air, falling back down to the ground with a biscuity crunch. Bogey clutched his winded stomach as he slid down the slimy carpet thread. As he started to wriggle free, the ginger wall of fluff began to move violently, jerking and spluttering. A choking noise could be heard and yet still Bogey could not work out what they were dealing with. Just then the ginger mound uprooted from the spot and rose high up into the air, still choking and coughing. Then another object appeared. This time it was an opening, a huge smelly opening with ginormous pointy-white fangs. A pongy, fishy, rotten smelling wind whizzed past Bogey's nostrils.

'Errrggghhh!!!' Bogey flinched from the awful rank odour of stale tuna.

'Er, Boges,' said Fluff, as she picked up Crumb and inched her way slowly backward.

'I'd make a move if I were you!' said Crumb. He too had twigged what was about to happen.

The choking and spluttering got louder and more agitated. The ginger mound twitched as the giant fishy mouth opened wide and out flew the most hideous furry ball of mucus and vomit, all balled up into one neat hairy fishy sphere, and heading straight for Bogey.

SPLAT! dribbled the giant sick-ball covering Bogey from head to toe in fishy gunk. Mucus, vomit, hair and old decaying fish bits smothered him completely.

Bogey didn't dare breathe as he tried to wriggle free. His arms and legs appeared from out of the enormous fur ball. Then two eyes popped open.

'Get me out of this quick!' came a muffled cry.

Bogey looked like a giant sick ball with arms and legs and the smell wafting from his general direction would make the bottom of any dustbin smell like a summer meadow.

'OOH... 'SCUSE ME... I AM SO SORRY, I DID'NT SEE YOU DOWN... YAWN!!!' came a very deep and lethargic voice.

Everyone looked up to see two giant brown eyes staring down at them, blinking with a friendly gaze, a speckled brown nose and a big beaming smile surrounded by mounds of ginger fur.

'Ginger Bags!' yelped Fluff in excitement, jumping on the spot, all the fluff on her back was standing to attention. Bogey and Crumb gaped up at the giant fluffy mound, their mouths wide open in disbelief.

'IT'S HART-LEY... FANK *YOU* VERY MUCH... GINGER BAGS! I ASK YOU, WHERE DO THEY... YAAAWWNNN! GET IT... YAWN!' Ginger Bags was a huge mound of baggy fluff, a ginger-tom-cat, constantly tired and inherently lazy. His yawns were so infectious he could put you to sleep in seconds... Sure enough Bogey and Crumb had started to yawn as they knelt down to rest their weary legs and within three and a half seconds precisely they were fast asleep dreaming of cake and chocolate.

'Oi! You two, wake up, don't leave me on my own!' shouted Fluff as she pushed Bogey, who in turn knocked over Crumb. They both woke up with a jolt.

'Do you know anything of the uprising Ginger… err… Hartley?' said Fluff, correcting herself, hoping for a profound and inspiring answer to their problems. But all she got was a giant rumbling sound as Ginger Bags, Bogey and Crumb fell back to sleep and snored very, very loudly.

CREAK, CLICK, THUD, THUMP… CREAK, CLICK, THUD THUMP!! Fluff, startled, quickly looked behind to see a dust cloud heading her way followed by a thousand shiny black creatures crawling from the Twisted Forest. She looked back to Ginger Bags to see appearing from beneath his orange fur a hundred or more clicking and crawling fleas. The ginger of his fur quickly turned to a black mass of creepy bodies, clambering over each other, all with one thing on their minds… to devour.

'Bogey, Crumb, wake up!' Fluff yelled at the top of her voice.

'They can't help ya now, my dear!' Appearing victorious on the cat's nose stood Crane, standing proud and invincible surrounded by his loyal and bloodthirsty army. Ginger Bags was infested with fleas, but it didn't stir him once.

'I claim this carpet on behalf of all fleas everywhere! Anyone who resists will be drained like the mites and the ants!' Crane held up a torn and blood stained cloak. It was Lord Itch.

Fluff held her hand to her mouth in fright. She felt utter dread in the pit of her stomach.

The tall hooded figure had only just got free of all the cat mucus as he started to edge his way gingerly into the Twisted Forest. Immediately the carpet threads sprung into action, grabbing hold of the spindly figure, the possessed tentacles spiralled around his feet, tripping him to the ground, they strangled and choked tighter and tighter around his body as he tried to wriggle free.

Just then the twisted carpet threads behind Fluff sprung into life, screaming with rage as they span like a web around her. Fluff had no time to run – she was trapped.

Crane and his flea army had infested the Magic Carpet and gained control of the Twisted Forest. Any creature that moved was strangled, drained of blood or pinned to the spot by the screaming carpet threads. Bogey and Crumb had succumbed too. They now lay fast asleep in a tangled woolly web, snoring in alternation. The uprising was over. The carpet was lost. Nobody could stop Crane now.

'Will ya get your butt out of my face!' yelled Dribble, trying to steady Smell, who was balancing on top of Dribble's shoulders in the murky darkness of the pit. Balancing on Smell's shoulders were the two dust mites, wobbling precariously trying to climb up the pit walls.

'It's no good, Dribble, I'm gonna have to use the Hover-pants, otherwise we'll never make it in time!' said Smell, itching to have another go on them. Just then the dust mites lost their balance and came crashing down, landing on top of Dribble and Smell.

'We can't risk it, bud, you're just not accurate enough!' said Dribble, picking himself up and scratching his head.

'What if I spin a web, click, and you grab on as I crawl up the wall, click!' said Fangs.

'Will ya have enough grip and will ya web be strong enough?' questioned Dribble.

'I'll have you know, click, web is one of the strongest things around!' Fangs began to spin a yard of web and threw it at the pit wall.

'There, try and break that!' he boasted. Smell and the mites grabbed hold of the web and pulled with all their might to break the sticky, elastic thread. But the tension was too much and they bounced off the pit wall and ended up in a tangled mess…

Fangs started to crawl up the wall, spinning at high speed as he inched his way slowly toward the Magic Carpet above. Every foot carefully searched for the best grip as the silver yarn grew from his back legs. Smell and the mites grabbed hold of the trailing web while Dribble stayed down holding onto the other end. His plan was to encourage all the carpet dwellers into the pit, away from the fleas, for a chance to start a new life away from all the fear and destruction that would follow. If the fleas wanted the carpet then maybe a new life could be found in the pit.

As Smell hung on for dear life, slipping occasionally on the luminous thread, he hoped Bogey and his friends hadn't forgotten him and would forgive him for behaving so badly. Hope and excitement pounded through his chest as they neared the Magic Carpet from below. Underneath the carpet dangled torn threads dangling through the gaps in the floorboards. Sharp rays of light pierced their way through, blinding Smell and the mites, but illuminating strange cocooned bodies that hung from the threads, lifeless and deformed with age…

'*Go back…*' whispered an eerie female voice inside Smell's head. Startled, he lost his grip, bounced off one of the mites and fell. Immediately Fangs' quick reflexes sprang into action, grabbing Smell around the waist. The mites yelled as the web stretched and creaked with the extra tension.

'Did you hear that?' cried Smell as he looked all around, spooked by the voice. It wasn't so much a real voice but a voice inside his head.

'*You must go back now or be dammed for eternity...*'

'Aaaarrrggghhh!!!' yelled Smell as he covered his ears in fear. Fangs tightened his grip on him.

'What are doing? *Click!*' yelled Fangs.

'Voices! Can't you hear them?'

'No?' Fangs looked around with his eight enormous eyes; seeing in the dark was a speciality of his.

'There's nothing there. Now stop wriggling or I'll drop you. *Click!*'

Just then the tension in the web became too much and part of it started to unravel, gaining speed as it spiralled out of control. Fangs quickly began spinning as fast as he could to fix the tear.

'*There's no future, no hope, no life beyond the pit...*' Another voice crept its way into Smell's thoughts, this time a male voice but just as haunting as the first.

'Make it go away!' cried Smell as he covered his eyes. He felt tormented and frightened as more voices spoke.

'*You're one of us now... join the masses and be one...*'

'*Join the masses and be one!*'

Suddenly from the blackness appeared a number of strange creatures with hideously deformed faces, whizzing past on an icy breeze. Each had a different twisted expression; they screamed and giggled as they floated around Smell. Suddenly one of Fangs' feet slipped and, with a jolt, he quickly steadied himself. The jolt sent a shock wave to his other foot and instantly Smell fell into the darkness... The translucent pale creatures immediately dived after him into the abyss. Fangs began to spin again faster than before. He rolled the web into a ball and threw it into the void below...

The web unravelled, jolted, then went limp. Fangs had missed him. He tried again and then again, but it was no use. Smell had gone. The silence drummed louder in the pit as Fangs and the mites listened...

Smell looked down between his little legs. As he fell, a musty warm breeze whizzed by his nostrils, taking his breath. There was no way of knowing how fast or which way he was falling. He strained to see anything in the dark but he could hear the wispy creatures following him from above, chattering and cooing as they chased him deeper into the blackened void. He blinked for a minute, as two eyes in the dark appeared right below him. He looked again, confused. Nothing. Suddenly they appeared again, this time to his left, eyes of emerald green and glowing intensely, starring up at him. A chilled shiver raced down Smell's spine. He rubbed his eyes, still falling but never catching up with the eyes in the dark. They seemed to be smiling at him. Smell closed his eyes and waited for the inevitable doom. Deeper and deeper he fell. It felt like he'd fallen deeper than the pit itself. Suddenly from the back of his mind he heard a dark demonic voice call out...

'UNDERPANTS!!'

Smell quickly opened his eyes in fright; the eyes in the dark had gone. He looked around as his heart pounded, trying to jump out of his chest.

'Underpants?' he questioned, rubbing his head. He was picking up speed and falling fast.

'Underpants!' he yelled, suddenly remembering his Hover-pants still stuffed inside his pocket. He quickly clambered in the darkness, fumbling to put them on straight. Immediately he whizzed into action, reversing course with a jolt.

'Out... of... control!' he yelled, doing a Superman impression, his hands out in front. Instantly he was catapulted with enormous speed upward and heading straight toward the Magic Carpet again.

Fangs squinted in the hazy darkness...

'There, look! What's that?' he cried, one of his spindly legs pointing to movement below. The mites were still dangling on the web ladder but could not see a thing. Suddenly an enormous gust of smelly wind blew past them as Captain Underpants hurtled out of control, crashed into Fangs and sent everyone up through the gap in the Magic Carpet, landing on the topside of Dribble's Leap.

Chapter Eleven

Itch

Back at the Twisted Forest, Crane's power had strengthened. All the carpet threads around him twitched with his will to devour and conquer. His body had doubled in size, swollen from the blood he'd consumed. He looked stronger and younger, a far cry from his frail former self. The mites had been exterminated. The ant army had all been wiped out and yet through all the fighting and chaos, Ginger Bags, Bogey and Crumb were still fast asleep, snoring like babies, oblivious to the impending doom. The hooded figure was now cocooned by the twisted threads of carpet and Fluff too was still trapped, only her face visible as the threads tightened. She tugged and pulled, trying to break free.

'It's no use, me pretty! The harder you tug the tighter the carpet becomes... You, like your friends, are now mine!' Crane cackled, drunk on power and blood. He moved closer to Fluff. She tried to step back but could not move an inch. Crane towered above her and roared a hideous screeching battle cry that could be heard echoing through the entire carpet; every flea instantly looked up to the sky and screeched in response. It was a deafening, blood curdling noise that sent Fluff into a dizzy faint. She fell to the floor and passed out…

Despite being unconscious, Fluff still felt conscious and was aware of her surroundings, or lack of them. She was no longer in the Twisted Forest; instead, she was now in a dark place. No light. No sense of space. Nothing except complete and utter silence. She tried to move, but she still felt trapped by the carpet threads that had ensnared her. Suddenly she felt something rough and painful on the side of her ncck. A warm rushing sensation pulsed through her head. She felt weak. She had an urge to panic and tried to struggle free from whatever had got hold of her in the dark. Just then she saw something in the gloom that stopped her struggling. Two eyes in the dark stared menacingly at her. They were wide-open and emerald green. Fluff tried to pull away but still she could not move.

'ITCH!' came a demonic voice in her head.

'What?' she questioned blinded by the intense glow from the eyes.

'ITCH!' bellowed the impatient voice again, this time louder. The eyes in the dark jumped forward then disappeared in a flash.

'Itch?' she thought, suddenly getting an urge to scratch her neck. Just then she felt one of her arms become free – she could moved it, so she quickly scratched her neck. It was painful, she felt something rough and warm and then she heard an almighty roar. Instantly her eyesight returned, she was back in the Twisted Forest, still trapped, lying on the floor. Above her was Crane. With blood dripping from his mouth, he roared again in pain. Fluff felt blood dripping down her neck.

'OOH, W-WHAT'S THAT YA SAID? I HAVEN'T 'AD THE KIPPERS!' Ginger Bags suddenly woke up and yawned. Crane looked up and yawned back, immediately falling to the ground in a drowsy slump.

'WHAT'S BEEN GOING ON ABOUT THE PLACE?' said Ginger Bags, scratching behind his left ear.

'OOH, THAT'S A RIGHT ONE THAT IS!' he bellowed, having another scratch, this time behind his right ear. He was still covered in fleas from head to toe. They swarmed his ginger coat, dulling his golden glow.

Realising she was free, Fluff quickly sprung to her feet with a rush, but something suddenly caught her eye. She looked around to see something enormous towering above her in the sky...

'AAAAHHHH!!!!' yelled Mum, who had walked into the spare room to get her sewing kit.

'AAAAHHHH!!!!' she screamed again, putting her hands to her mouth.

'FLEAS!!!!' She quickly disappeared out of the room.

Crane found his balance and rose to his feet again, looking even more menacing and very angry indeed. He crawled toward Fluff; one of her feet was still trapped by the twisted carpet, it spiralled around her leg and tightened fast. Blood dripped from Crane's mouth as he leant forward to take another bite.

Finally Bogey and Crumb started to stir as the flea army closed in for the kill. Ginger Bags could not stop scratching behind his ears, under his legs, the tip of his nose and the end of his tail. The fleas swarmed his entire body driving him insane.

'OOOHHH!!! GET 'EM OFF, THEY'RE BITING ME WOTSITS!' he yelled, trying to satisfy a million itches at once. Bogey woke up and yawned at the commotion, nudging Crumb who was still snoozing. Bogey looked up at Fluff wearing a puzzled expression on his face. She realised he wasn't looking at her, but behind. She turned around to see an enormous rectangular object heading straight toward them…

WHOOOOOOOSSSSHHH!!!!!!!

An almighty gust of wind sucked everything up in its path. The twisted carpet threads were yanked straight upright, standing to attention. Dust and debris whizzed towards the rectangular object. There was no resisting its power as thousands of fleas flew into the air and disappear yelling and screaming, clicking and creaking.

Crane quickly grabbed hold of Fluff's free arm as he was yanked up into the air, his legs trailing behind him he struggled to hold on. A whirlwind had started picking up everything in its path. The hooded figure was also holding on for dear life as the wind grew stronger and stronger. His cloak flapped and tugged with the intense force. Suddenly the cloak lifted up into the air and flew into the sky, revealing the strange creature beneath. Or should I say strange creatures beneath?

Hiccup!

Holding onto a torn thread of carpet were two familiar figures... Herron and Finch! Herron was strapped to Finch's shoulders and Finch had a pair of wooden stilts strapped to his legs. Crane looked over at the two scrawny traitors and screamed an almighty roar. Herron and Finch bowed their heads in shame. They'd been defrocked. They braced themselves for the inevitable outcome of such treachery... death! The wind intensified, turning the whirlwind into a giant vortex. Suddenly the vortex took hold of Crane, sucking him up and away into the dust cloud that swirled above like a giant sea creature. He screamed one last scream as he disappeared through the jaws of the storm. The storm roared with satisfaction.

Ginger Bags had managed to claw into the Magic Carpet for grip, the fleas that had once swarmed all over him were now gone. Bogey and Crumb were slowly being unravelled from the carpet too. Suddenly Fluff lost her grip and flew into the vortex with immense speed.

'Fluff!' yelled Bogey as he let go of the Magic Carpet, whizzing into the mouth of the giant whirlwind. Crumb immediately let go too, grabbing hold of Bogey's leg as they flew round and round, higher and higher. Crumb caught a glimpse of Bogey, who had managed to grab hold of Fluff. Herron and Finch could no longer hold on, and they too were catapulted into the funnel of wind. No creature could resist the ferocity of the gusty beast. They whooshed through the air in a whirlwind of debris and carpet bits. Everything from frying pans to underpants flew into the air with them. High above the Magic Carpet they travelled, away from the Twisted Forest, over Dribble's Leap and beyond. Fluff was out in front and could make out the shadow of something ahead. She squinted to see through the storm – the shape looked familiar. It got closer and closer until suddenly her nose was pressed up against it.

'AAARRRGGGHHH!!!' it yelled.

'Smell!' cried Fluff as she tried to manoeuvre her nose away from his butt.

'Fluff!' cried Smell in excitement.

'How did you get here?' she cried, trying to grab hold of him.

'We made it back to Dribble's Leap, then got sucked into the vortex!' he yelled. Fluff could only just hear him. Smell was holding onto the two dust mites out in front.

'Look who's behind me!' she cried. Smell looks behind to see his old pal, a sight he thought he'd never see again.

'Boges!!' he screamed with joy. A beaming happy grin lights up his face.

'What have you gone and done this time?' Bogey cried out, trying to hide his joy. Secretly he was overwhelmed to see his best friend again, but he'd never let on. Fluff, Smell, Bogey, Crumb and the mites hurtled through the air followed by Herron and Finch, who had started arguing about whose fault all this was. The wind took their breath away as they climbed even higher when suddenly something came into view that put the fear of dread into Fluff, Bogey and Crumb.

'AAARRRGGGHHH!!!' What's that?' screamed Bogey, as a number of black hairy legs appear before them.

'Oh, that's Fangs!' said Smell.

'He helped us out of the pit!'

'Hellllow!' said Fangs. Eight black eyes stared down on them, his front claws opened and closed with intrigue.

''Ello.' said Bogey politely, trying to keep away from his giant pointy teeth. One minute they were running for their lives away from the enormous hairy beast, the next they were flying through the air at a hundred miles an hour exchanging pleasantries. Fangs smiled a big, cheesy grin at Bogey, his eyes bulging and his fangs glistening.

'ARRGGHH!!!' yelled Bogey. Fangs chuckled to himself.

'Grab hold of one of my legs!' he yelled. Everyone quickly obliged. They flew high above the Magic Carpet, swirling around and around.

'I think I'm gonna be sick!' yelled Bogey clutching his big belly with one arm. He'd gone very green indeed. All sorts of bits and pieces whizzed by them at high speed: the heads of Jelly Babies, arms of chocolate cookies. Bogey thought he saw their little green Monopoly house spiralling out of control and even one of Mrs Mite's strawberry blonde wigs went hurtling by at great velocity.

Suddenly something crashed into them, bouncing off the two dust mites. Smell almost lost his grip but managed to quickly grab onto another leg. The two dust mites weren't so lucky. Fangs quickly extended a spare leg to try to save them, but it was no use - they flew off so fast and hurtled upward into the vortex.

'Look! It's Crane!' yelled Fluff, pointing at the twisted body whirling around before them. He was spinning out of control and screaming as he went.

'I'll get you, if it's the last thing I do!' he screamed with such venom, his blood-red eye fixed on Fluff. Suddenly the wind dropped and everyone fell dramatically toward the carpet.

'AAARRRGGGHHH!!!' everyone screamed as they plummeted out of the sky.

The dust was settling fast as Mum leant the vacuum cleaner up against the wall to inspect her handiwork.

'There. Clean and tidy! I will not have fleas in this house!' she said as she left the spare room, clapping her hands together, clearly satisfied with a job well done. Not a flea, not a bug, not a creepy crawly and not even a speck of dust was in sight. Until…

'AAARRRGGGHHH!!!'

CRASH!!! BANG!!! WOLLOP!!! Fangs came crashing back down to the Magic Carpet, followed by Smell, Bogcy, Fluff and Crumb, all landing on top of each other.

'We're back home!' yelled Bogey, jumping for joy at the sight of the little green Monopoly house standing before them.

'AARRGGHH!'

CRASH! BANG! WOLLOP! as Herron and Finch bounced off the roof of Smell and Bogey's little green house and landed in their front garden, knocking down the fence.

Smell picked himself up and walked over to inspect the tiny green Monopoly house. It had survived the storm – the doors and windows were gone and the house looked a little wonky, but it was still standing. So too was Fluff's house next door.

Fluff stood up and listened to the silence in the Magic Carpet. It was the first time in a long while she'd heard so much quiet. It was peaceful and calm. The Magic Carpet felt like home again.

After a lot of catching up and story telling, Fangs, Fluff, Bogey, Smell and Crumb sat down to interrogate Herron and Finch.

'We had to do something. *Hiccup*!' begged Finch.

'Yeah, they'd been breeding an army for years. We had to warn you somehow and get you to leave!' said Herron, his forehead pulsing with the rush of blood.

'This was our home too, remember? They wanted to infest the entire carpet. Nothing would've stood a chance! The flea army takes no prisoners.' Despite Herron and Finch being fleas, they were pretty bad at being fleas. They'd never caused any problems in the past and they'd lived topside of the Magic Carpet for a number of years. Everyone agreed that Herron and Finch posed no threat and were welcomed as friends. Fangs the spider said his goodbyes to Smell and the others. His belly had shrunk to nothing and he was in desperate need of a square meal. He promised Smell that he would always be there if he should ever need a friend. And with an eight legged wave, he crawled off into the sunset.

After a lot of tidying up, Bogey made tea and hot buttered crumpets for everyone. The crumpets stayed on the plate long enough to be eaten this time and everyone was happy. Little Crumb was welcomed officially and Fluff offered to put him up in her house next door. That made Smell slightly jealous, but after all they'd been through, he wasn't about to make a fuss.

That evening, as the dust settled back on the Magic Carpet, Smell packed away his Hover-pants in his top drawer and sat on his bed and breathed a sigh of relief.

'What an adventure,' he thought as he began to drift off. But one thing played on his mind… Dribble. Should he tell Fluff he'd met Dribble in the pit? A million questions whizzed through his mind as his feet started to twitch. Had Dribble survived the storm? Who had spoken to him in the pit with the green eyes? And what had happened to Crane? Smell fell fast asleep almost instantly as night fell in the Magic Carpet.

Outside everything was calm and still. New dust and debris had settled on the ground ready to spring into new life. Across the darkened room a blue hazy glow shone, bouncing off the tops of the carpet threads… Suddenly there was movement in the dark by the vacuum cleaner, which was still leaning up against the spare room wall. Creeping silently out from the now dormant machine were two black legs.

They stretched, creaking and clicking as the figure straightened its twisted body and crept into the shadows. One blood-red eye stared back at the green Monopoly house in rage. The creature turned its back and crawled into the night…

Smell & Bogey will return in… 'Smell & Bogey and the Missing Slippers.'

Lightning Source UK Ltd.
Milton Keynes UK
UKOW02f1806070315

247472UK00001B/12/P